OPERATOR 5:
WAR-MASTERS FROM THE ORIENT

WAR-MASTERS
FROM THE ORIENT

By Curtis Steele

STEEGER BOOKS • 2020

PUBLISHING HISTORY

"War-Masters from the Orient" originally appeared in the March, 1936 (Vol. 6, No.
    4) issue of *Operator #5* magazine. Copyright © 2020 by Argosy Communications,
    Inc. All rights reserved.

FOREWORD

C OLD RUSSIAN sun glinted on desolate, shell-torn fields. Here and there lay the still-smoldering debris of a wooden house which had been struck by roaring projectiles.

Along the narrow, white road which paralleled the torn-up, single-track railroad lay the bodies of gray-clad Soviet soldiers, torn and maimed. Rifles, knapsacks, canteens, various articles of clothing also lay strewn along the way. At the side of the road, a gun-carriage tilted crazily in the ditch, the gun pointing grotesquely at a sign on the opposite side which had miraculously survived the punishing barrage that must have been laid down upon the road not so long before. The sign read:

MOSCOW—220 *verstya* ↦

↤ LENINGRAD—300 *verstya*

An old Model T Ford touring car chugged over a rise from the direction of Moscow. Its radiator was smoking. Icicles clung to the windshield and to the outsides of the curtains, which were carefully locked on to keep out the cold.

A thin man was driving, and beside him sat a girl of perhaps twenty or twenty-one. They were both clothed in astrakhan coats and caps with earmuffs. They wore heavy, fur-lined gloves. Their faces were red from the biting cold, and the girl's eyes were watering.

1

The driver was hunched forward over the wheel, and each time he expelled his breath, a huge cloud of vapor issued from between his lips, as if he were smoking. His face was thin, pinched; and at intervals a twinge of agony crossed his features, and he put a hand quickly to his side, where blood seeped through his coat and stained the fur.

At the top of the rise, abreast of the sign, he pressed his foot on the brake, brought the car to a squealing stop. The girl

It was the greatest disaster in American naval history.

glanced at him swiftly, put a hand on his arm, spoke with quick sympathy.

"Feodor! Your wound makes you weak! Let me drive!"

Feodor smiled bitterly. "It is hopeless, Katerina," he answered, in the full, guttural accents of Southern Russia, in which the girl had also spoken. He pointed to the signpost. "It is three hundred versts farther to Leningrad. The Russian armies have retreated all the way. Behind us come the tanks and the motorcycles of the Asiatic hordes. We cannot hope to outdistance them!"

Weakly, as if every move caused excruciating agony, he opened the side door, stood in the road. The girl descended from the other side of the car and joined him, looking back over the empty expanse through which they had come. Far in the distance, the sunlight glinted on metal.

Feodor raised a hand and pointed. "There they come, Katerina. They move twice—no, three times—as fast as we. There is no chance to escape them!"

Katerina's beautiful, finely chiseled features were raw from the cold. Her black eyes flashed.

"Feodor!" she exclaimed. "You must not give up like this!" The patrician lines of her face hardened, set stubbornly. "Come, Feodor. Let us go on. There may yet be a chance—"

He shook his head. His eyes were on the metallic flashes far back on the road. "See," he said, "the vanguard of the Leopard's hosts will soon be upon us. Those armored motorcycles could have caught us long ago, but the Leopard is playing with us—he knows he will get us. He knows there is no help for us between here and Leningrad." His thin lips tightened. "While Europe drains itself of life in war, these hordes overrun Russia. And you and I, sister, are the only ones who know what the Leopard plans next. If we die here, both of us, there will be no one to warn the world—"

She tugged at his arm, her insistence becoming more frantic as the glinting metal ranks drew ever nearer. Now she could make out the individual shapes of the armored motorcycles

4

which seemed to be flying toward them with the speed of rockets.

"All the more reason for us to escape. Come, Feodor—!"
GENTLY HE pushed her hand from his arm, moved to the car, and reached inside. From within he brought out a submachine gun, lifting the heavy weapon with a tremendous effort. The stain on his coat grew larger as he adjusted a clip in the gun.

"What are you going to do, Feodor?" the girl asked, suddenly breathless.

He looked at her, smiled gravely. "Both of us have no chance to escape, Katerina. One of us has. Get in the car, and drive. It is only thirty miles to where the plane is hidden. I will hold the Leopard here—for a while."

The girl's cheeks paled. "No, no, Feodor! You will be killed—"

"Exactly. I am dying anyway. I will stay here and stop them for a little while. It will give you a start—"

"No! Let me surrender to the Leopard. He will not harm me, and he will spare you if I give myself up to him. It is I whom he wants—"

"Stop!" Feodor's voice was like the crack of a whip. There was a terrible anger in his eyes, and for a moment it seemed as if he would strike her. Then his voice softened. "Katerina," he said urgently, "remember that you are a Saratoff. Remember that your father was a Duke of the Russian Empire. Rather than see you give yourself to this Leopard—this coolie who has made himself the master of Asia—I would shoot you with my own hand. You must go, Katerina. In Leningrad, you will find Captain Kusmarenko. He will take you in his steamer to America. There, you will find this friend of mine, whose name I have given you—James Christopher. He is known as Operator 5 of the American Intelligence. You will tell him you are my sister. He will remember me. Give him the paper which you carry. Make him understand what the Leopard plans. He will know what to do."

Feodor turned from her toward the swiftly approaching motorcycles.

"Go quickly, Katerina. In a moment it will be too late."

"I will stay with you," she announced stubbornly.

HE DID not look at her. "Go!" he repeated harshly, as he knelt in the road, raising the submachine gun, resting it on one knee. "In your hands rests the fate of the world. You have no choice!"

For a moment she stood there, looking down at him rebelliously. The motorcycles were less than a mile away. The road was filled with them, and far behind them she could see horsemen. Great clouds of dust rose in the air from the advancing host.

Feodor said over his shoulder: "Katerina, I am the head of the family. You swore to our father before he died that you would obey me in all things. You swore it by the Holy Virgin, and you kissed the cross. Will you violate that oath now?"

He could not see the anguish in her eyes, but he heard the choked sob that caught in her throat.

"I—will go, Feodor," she said, very low. "I obey."

He sighed, his eyes still on the advancing motorcycles, which

6

had slowed down now, at sight of them. "There are more clips of ammunition in the car," he told her, matter-of-factly. "Leave them beside me."

Moving as in a dream, she took out four clips, placed them next to him, then bent impulsively and threw her arms around him. "Feodor!" she cried brokenly. "I can't bear to leave you here to die—"

He laughed grimly, lifting his eyes to her. "The Saratoffs know how to die, Katerina."

She kissed him. "Good-by, Feodor. I will go to America, and find this friend of yours, this Operator 5. And I swear to you that I will never rest until I have seen the Leopard pay for the Saratoff blood he is about to spill!"

She said it calmly enough, but there was a queer, cold deadness in her voice. He pressed her hand, pushed her away.

She got into the car, the motor of which had been left running. She pressed the pedal, and the old Ford pulled away, leaving Feodor Saratoff in the road facing the speeding motorcycles….

HE DID not look after her, did not wave. Tight-lipped, he stretched out, belly to the ground, and sighted along the submachine gun. He heard the Ford chugging away, and above it the quick back-firing of the oncoming motorcycles. There were perhaps fifty of them, and they advanced two abreast on the narrow road. Each was equipped with an armored side-car, from which projected the muzzle of a gun.

The thundering cycles swept up the rise in the road toward where Saratoff lay, and he pressed the trip of his gun, sent a stream of lead screaming toward them. He aimed low, at a point beneath the metal plates which protected the drivers of the two foremost machines.

His slugs clanged against steel, and the two first motorcycles careened madly, crashed into each other with a deafening explosion, in the center of the road. Tongues of flame lanced up from them, and in a second the second pair of cycles had piled upon the first, adding to the twisted, blazing wreckage.

The cycles behind swerved sharply to avoid the same fate, spreading out to either side of the road, and slowing to a halt.

Feodor Saratoff, grinning coldly behind the sights of his machine gun, kept up a steady stream of lead, fanning it across from one side of the road to the other. But now, with the motorcycles halted, his barrage did little damage. His first burst had caught the only exposed portion of the bodies of the drivers—their feet. The following cyclists had drawn their feet up behind the protection of the armor plates, and there was now nothing to shoot at. The screaming lead from the machine gun clanged futilely against the metal armor.

Strangely enough, the muzzles of the guns which peeped from the loopholes in the armor of each of those motorcycles did not spit death back at the prone man on the hilltop. On the contrary, they were silent.

Saratoff emptied his clip, frenziedly slipped another into the hot gun. In the quarter-minute that it took him to effect the change, the cycles chugged another fifty feet toward him, then stopped again as he let loose another burst, which did no harm.

Behind the cycles, a company of cavalry was cantering up, and the troops stopped, just out of range. Then, at an order from an officer, they fanned out into the fields on either side of the road, and advanced warily in a flanking movement, still staying out of range. Not a single shot had yet been fired at the lone man.

Saratoff wavered to his feet, holding the still chattering machine gun at his hip. He swung it in a wide arc, so that his slugs now cut a wide swathe into the fields on both sides. He could see where his snub-nosed bullets plowed into the ground, far short of the troops, and he cursed wildly, feverishly inserted another clip. The hot breech burned his hands through the gloves. In the brief respite while he ceased firing, the motorcycles moved forward once more, stopped immediately when he again pressed the trip of the gun. The cavalry remained out of range.

Saratoff glanced fleetingly behind him, smiled thinly as he saw that the road toward Leningrad was empty as far as the eye could reach. The old Ford was out of sight. He turned and bared his teeth at the sight of the motorcycles, which had stolen another fifty feet. He shouted wild defiance into the air.

"You want me alive, Mr. Leopard! Well, come and take me!"

And once more the staccato chattering of his machine gun cut through the air, and the motorcycles halted.

He had only one clip left on the ground beside him. The bloodstain in his right side was spreading over his coat, and dripping to the ground to form a small crimson pool. His face was pinched with frost, though his hands were hot from contact with the gun.

He could see the horsemen, crouching low over their mounts, waiting for him to exhaust his ammunition before charging in. These men wore strange, angularly shaped helmets, and breastplates of some sort of chain mesh which bent with their bodies. The horses were unprotected, and that was why the riders kept out of range.

Grimly he played the mad tune on his gun, finished the clip, and reloaded. Once more the motorcycles rolled up toward him, stopped when he started to fire again. This was the last clip. Behind the motorcycles and the cavalry, marching foot soldiers appeared on the road, helmeted and mailed. They were marching four abreast, and their armor shone in the sun. In the forefront of the infantry, a banner eddied in the slight breeze, billowed out, showing a white background upon which was emblazoned the figure of a leopard, stretched at full length, apparently leaping through the air.

A FIGURE became visible, cantering ahead of that banner. It was a mounted man, riding a tall, coal-black horse. Saratoff's eyes, glued to his sights, glinted with hatred as he glimpsed that horseman. He was naked, save for a loin cloth. Naked, in that frozen country where no man dared venture out unless bundled in furs! Saratoff raised the sights of the gun, sent lead screaming over the heads of the cavalry. His burst fell far short, but the naked rider seemed to recognize the gesture, and raised one arm in a mocking salute.

Now, Feodor's last clip was exhausted. His gun became silent, and he threw the smoking weapon from him, reached into his coat pocket and drew out a heavy automatic. He stood with this in his hand—legs braced wide, tottering upon his feet with the blood from his side dripping slowly to the ground—and faced the advancing array of mailed men.

His face was set grim with hatred, as the motor-cycles once more resumed their advance, and the horsemen began closing  in from both sides. He fired nine times in rapid succession, swinging his gun from side to side. Horses fell with each shot but in a moment he was hemmed in, the last shot fired from his automatic.

Mailed men leaped from the horses and from behind the armored plates of the motorcycles. Saratoff's fists flailed out in fierce resistance, but his arms were seized, and he was held helpless. The faces of his captors were not visible behind their glittering metal helmets, but almond eyes peered out at him through slitted eyeholes as his struggles stopped. He stood, breathing hard, would have fallen were it not for the hands that held him up.

The press about him opened, and the naked man on the black horse rode up close and dismounted, stood facing Saratoff.

The naked man towered above the frail Russian. He was a giant of a man, with muscles that played in powerful ripples over all his body and that ridged his back. He was a Chinese, and his skin was dark, oily. His face was broad, flat, distinctly Mongol, with thick lips and high cheekbones. His hair was cropped close to his head, and his eyes were surmounted by bushy, unkempt brows. The lips were parted now, in a cruel smile of vindictiveness. He spoke in a queer, high-pitched dialect of the Steppes.

"Saratoff, I promised I would kill you with these two hands if you tried to escape with your sister!"

Feodor Saratoff raised his head, not attempting any longer to struggle in the grip of his captors. He answered simply: "I am ready to die, Leopard!"

The naked man turned, spoke swift orders to a mailed officer who stood behind him, using the sing-song Cantonese dialect.

The officer saluted, stepped back, and raised a hand, issued orders to the crews of the motorcycles. At once, the men returned to their machines, started the motors, and set off down the road in the direction the Ford had taken.

The naked man turned back to Saratoff, who smiled defiantly. "You will not catch her, Leopard. By this time, she has reached a plane which we had hidden in Novomirsk!"

The features of the naked man contorted with rage. Stained teeth showed through parted, thick, red lips. For a moment, those two slanted eyes flared in small, ruby pinpoints. Then the huge man seemed to master himself. He said coldly:

"She cannot go far enough, Saratoff. I will have her if I must comb the world. Just as you see the armies of Russia retreat before me, so shall the armies of other countries make way before me. Wherever she may hide, the Leopard will find her. Your sister, Saratoff, shall be the Leopard's queen! Where has she gone in the plane?"

Feodor Saratoff's eyes blazed. His whole body shook in futile anger. Far down on the road he could see rank upon rank of mailed men, marching. The hosts of Asia were behind this naked man in the loin-cloth. His body stiffened, and he threw his shoulders back, raised his head. He spoke slowly, with an apparent effort to remain calm.

"You are nothing but a filthy wharf-rat, Leopard—a filthy coolie who has somehow made himself master of Asia. But ruler of Asia or not, the Saratoffs are too good for you. My ancestors were Dukes of Muscovy while yours groveled in the mud of Mongolia. How dare you raise your eyes to a woman of the Saratoffs—you, in whose veins runs the hybrid blood of the carrion races of Asia!"

THE NAKED man snarled, stretched out two powerful, hairy hands toward Feodor's throat. But he stopped, suddenly laughed.

"You are clever, Saratoff. You wish to goad me into killing you before I force you to tell me where your sister has fled!" He shook his head. "It does not matter what you say of me. It remains that I am the master of Asia." He nodded. "Yes, a dirty coolie, raised on the waterfront of Mukden, now rules Asia. Soon he will rule the world. Look at these hands. They have loaded freight on a hundred boats, have stoked coal in a hundred engine rooms. Now they hold the fate of Asia. One day they will hold that beautiful sister of yours. It is my misfortune, Saratoff, that I once saw your sister. Now I must have this proud daughter of the Dukes of Muscovy; I will make her the queen of the dirty coolie who will rule the world. And now, Saratoff, you will tell me where she has fled."

Feodor laughed. "You are mistaken, Leopard. You think your tortures will make me talk. But a Saratoff knows how to endure pain. Once I was tortured by the Ogpu for four days, but I did

Dr. Fu held the vial under Feodor's nose....

not reveal the secrets of the White Russian army. Do you think I will betray my own sister?"

The Leopard nodded. "I think you will, Saratoff." He gestured at the torn-up fields on both sides of them. "Why do you think the Soviet armies retreated before me? They were as well armed and as numerous as my own forces. I will show you, Saratoff, why they retreated—and why you will tell me where your sister has gone."

He motioned behind him, spoke in Cantonese. A mailed horseman turned, and spurred down the road, alongside the ranks of troops. In a few moments, he returned with another rider. This was an old, wizened Chinese who carried a large, flat, black case under his arm.

The old man dismounted, bowed low before the naked one.

"Doctor Fu," said the Leopard, motioning toward Feodor, "I want this man to talk!"

Doctor Fu bowed once more, opened his case and drew a small vial from it. He came and stood before Feodor, spoke sharply to the two soldiers who held him: "Grip him tight. Do not let him move."

Then he removed the stopper from the vial, held it under Feodor's nose. Feodor tried to rear back, sudden panic in his eyes. But he was held firmly, helpless.

After a moment, Doctor Fu replaced the stopper in the vial, put the glass tube back in the case, and bowed again. "He will talk now, Lord," said the old doctor, and backed away.

The Leopard nodded, pleased, his gaze on Feodor. The thin

Russian's eyes were becoming glazed, dull. His jaw sagged a little. His feet slid a bit in the frozen puddle of his own blood.

The Leopard asked him softly: "Where did your sister, Katerina, fly in the plane, Saratoff?"

And suddenly, inexplicably, Feodor answered! He spoke in a dull voice, the words coming from his lips effortlessly, as if it were imperative that he tell: "She flies to Leningrad. There she will embark with a Captain Kusmarenko, who served our father, but who is now in the employ of the Soviet Steamship Lines. He will take her to America."

"And where will she be in America, Saratoff?"

"She seeks an old friend of mine, whom I knew in Constantinople. He is of the American Secret Service. He is known as Operator 5. His name is James Christopher."

The Leopard's ugly face darkened. He took a step closer. "She has a message, perhaps, for this James Christopher?"

"She has. I gave her a letter, stating everything that I discovered about you and your plans. It tells that you have some strange means of winning victory after victory in the field. It tells how you mastered Asia, and how you waited, watching Europe destroy itself in this new world war which is even more destructive than the first. It tells how you march across Russia to the sea."

"And do you also write to this Operator 5 of what I plan next?"

FEODOR NODDED dully. "I told him in the letter, how you plan to seize ships and sail for America with this strange power of yours that brings you victory always. And I warned

16

him that he must use all his ingenuity if he would prevent his country from becoming vassal to the Leopard of Asia."

The Leopard bent forward eagerly, asked tensely: "This power of mine, Saratoff—did you tell him what it was?"

"No. How could I? I do not know its nature myself."

The Leopard nodded in satisfaction. "That is so. I just wanted to make sure."

He turned to an officer behind him. "You heard, Dato?"

The mailed and helmeted officer bowed. "I heard, Lord."

"Then ride back at once. Send wires to our men in America. Have them watch the docks in every port. Find out what ship this Kusmarenko commands. We cannot reach Leningrad before her, but we can stop her at the docks in America. Also let our own men in America turn their attention to this Operator 5. You understand?"

The officer bowed. "I understand, Lord; and I obey." He clicked his heels, turned, and went to one of the motorcycles. In a moment, the cycle was turned around, and went speeding back up the road, along the ranks of halted soldiers.

The Leopard faced Feodor once more. There was a set smile of savagery on his broad, flat face. "And now, Saratoff," he laughed, "I keep my promise!" His two huge hands came up slowly to Feodor's throat, linked themselves around it, and pressed....

CHAPTER 1
THE LEOPARD MAKES A MOVE

I T WAS the seventh month after the entry of the United States into the Second World War, as it was already officially termed. Two million eight hundred thousand stalwart young Americans had been equipped with arms, hastily trained, and shipped across the Atlantic to bolster up the cracking battle-line of the League of Nations Sanctioning Powers. Materials of war had poured across the ocean in equally amazing quantities.

In seven months, the United States had stripped herself of men and materials in order—as the propagandists put it this time—"to make the world safe for Liberty!"

So cleverly had foreign diplomacy maneuvered—so brilliantly had foreign-financed propaganda played its cards—that the objections of those veterans who still recalled the tortured days and nights of the trenches of 1917 had been smothered under a wave of high-pitched national feeling.

America was plunged into the war....

A regiment of fresh conscripts was marching down Broadway to the accompaniment of blaring bands and the raucous cheers of the thousands who lined the curbs. From every window of the tall buildings on either side of New York's great thorough-fare, bits of paper and confetti fluttered down upon the marching men.

At the docks, four huge transports were waiting to take them aboard, together with other regiments which were hastily leav-

ing to plug up the gaps in the Twelfth
Division on the Southern Front.

In the Hudson River, eight huge
ships of war rode at anchor. These were
to be the convoys for the transports.
There were six long, sleek cruisers, and
the capital ships, *Dakota* and *Oregon*.
The *Dakota* was the flagship of the Atlantic fleet, and Admiral
Stanley Winston, who was going across to take command of
the Mediterranean blockade for the Sanctioning Powers, would
soon board her.

At Broadway and Forty-Second Street a black limousine
purred at the corner waiting for a break in the ranks of the
marching draftees so that it could proceed west.

The man at the wheel was pockmarked, with gnarled, bony
hands and a face upon which there was a set expression of stolid-
ity. He wore a chauffeur's cap and uniform, but his bearing was
far from being that of a servant.

In the rear of the car sat a man and a woman. The man was
grossly fat, and small eyes peered furtively out from between
folds of flesh. There was a queer, unhealthy color in his cheeks.
His companion was taller than he. Her dark hair was braided
around her head, and set off as in a frame by the high collar of
her ermine coat. Her red lips formed a bright line of color in her
otherwise white face. The coat was open at the throat, revealing
a string of shimmering pearls which lay across her breast.

The woman, as well as the two men, was quite distinctly of
Eastern origin. A keen observer might have placed them as

19

belonging to one of those Eurasian races of mixed European and Asiatic descent—which are notoriously known to have bred the most unprincipled spies and intriguers in history.

At the feet of the fat man and the woman, a bundle lay stretched across the floor of the car, covered by an auto robe. This bundle was wriggling frantically, and for a moment the robe was thrown back, revealing a young, freckled-faced boy, whose arms were tied behind his back, and who was cruelly gagged with a greasy automobile rag thrust into his mouth and tied behind his head with a luggage strap.

The boy's eyes expressed desperate anger as he labored to a half-sitting position, and tried to wriggle himself still higher.

The woman, who had been staring straight ahead at the marching men, over the shoulder of the chauffeur, glanced down and saw the struggles of the boy. She nudged her companion, said:

"That brat is up again, Dmitri. Someone will notice him while we are stopped here."

She spoke in English, with a slight trace of soft, slurring accent. Her beautiful features showed no tinge of emotion at the lad's pitiful struggles.

The fat man stirred, and frowned. He said nothing, but raised a foot, planted the sole squarely in the boy's face, and pushed. The bound lad's head cracked against the floor with a thud, and he lay still.

AT THAT moment the marching men halted, and a traffic officer motioned to the limousine to proceed. The chauffeur shifted into first, and shot the car across, then sped west toward the Hudson.

The woman said chidingly to the fat man beside her: "It will be too bad if you have cracked the boy's skull. We will need to have him conscious for a while, Dmitri."

Dmitri grunted, bent over and pinched the lad's pallid face. The boy uttered a muffled groan through the gag, and his eyes opened wide. The fat fingers had left a livid mark on his cheek.

Dmitri laughed. "You needn't worry," he said to the woman. "This boy is hard to kill—like his friend."

The boy glared up at his tormentor.

The woman looked down at him coldly, and remarked to her companion: "He has a lot of spirit; he will be hard to break."

"We'll break him, all right," the man chuckled. "We've broken harder ones."

Playfully he raised his foot again, poked his toe at a spot in the boy's elbow. The young captive squirmed in agony, and the fat man's chuckle rose higher.

"You see, Lina, my dear, there is a good deal of science to this business. One must use finesse. My toe poked him in what these Americans call the funny bone. Just a little tap, and you see the agony it causes. There are many little spots like that in the human body. I assure you this boy will not be able to resist my—er—persuasion for long."

The woman's gray-green, expressionless eyes regarded the fat man for a moment, and she shuddered. "I should hate, Dmitri, to be the subject of your attentions," she said. "It is not wise to have you for an enemy."

Dmitri bowed. "Thank you, Lina," he murmured. "Let us hope that the Leopard will appreciate my services when the time comes for dispensing rewards."

At Eleventh Avenue, the limousine swung onto the ramp leading to the elevated express highway, sped north to Riverside Drive, then up the Drive to One Hundred and Third Street. It pulled up before a brownstone house around the corner from the Roerich Museum. In the first floor window of this house was a modest sign which read:

DMITRI OSMAN
STUDIO OF THE DANCE

Cold wind roared in from the Hudson, causing pedestrians to walk with their heads down, more occupied in holding onto their hats than in watching the queer bundle which Dmitri and the chauffeur carried into the house.

The door was opened without their ringing by a skinny Oriental in a white house jacket, who grinned knowingly at sight of the squirming bundle, and lent a hand to the two men in carrying it into a room at the rear of the long, dark hall. The woman followed them in.

The room which they entered was darkened; there were two windows, but heavy steel shutters allowed no light to filter in. The walls were bare, and the only furniture was a cot with a single chair beside it, and a desk in one corner.

Dmitri and the chauffeur dumped the boy on the cot while the woman lit a cigarette and watched dispassionately.

Then the chauffeur, at a nod from the fat man, untied the

lad's hands, and removed the gag. He stepped back, drawing from a shoulder holster an automatic which he trained on the youthful prisoner.

THE BOY sat up on the cot with an effort, moved his arms, painfully, in order to restore circulation. He gazed from one to the other of his captors, and his young, freckled face wrinkled in perplexity. Finally he let his glance settle on the fat man and said:

"Maybe you'll tell me what's the big idea of the kidnapping, mister?"

Dmitri stepped close to him, brought his fat, pudgy hand down in a vicious, open-handed slap that stung the boy's cheek to a vivid purple hue.

"You will answer questions," he purred, "and not ask them."

The boy was flung back on the cot by the force of the blow. He did not cower, but lay there, glaring up at the other.

Dmitri bent over him. "Your name," he grated, "is Tim Donovan. You are the boy who assists the man known as Operator 5. You are his constant companion. I want to know if he has recently received a visit from a young lady named Katerina Saratoff." He bent lower, his eyes fastened on the boy's. "Well?"

The lad's cheek still stung from the vicious blow. He pressed his lips tight to keep back the tears that came involuntarily to his eyes, and suddenly raised his knees, kicked upward with both feet. The heels of his shoes caught the fat man in the stomach, and Dmitri was thrown backward, doubled up in agony, both hands pressed to his paunch.

The boy grinned, shouted: "That's for the smack you took at my funny bone, Fatty! Maybe—"

He got no further, for the stocky, pockmarked chauffeur had rushed in with his automatic clubbed. He brought the butt down on the boy's head, and the youngster buckled over on the cot, unconscious. Blood oozed from his scalp at the spot where the gun-butt had struck. He twitched a moment, then lay still.

The fat man was groaning with pain. He backed into the chair, leaned far forward, still clutching at his stomach, swaying from side to side, and moaning loudly.

The woman paid no attention to the fat man, but hurried to the cot, put a hand on the boy's heart. After a second she nodded, then turned to the chauffeur, her eyes flashing.

"You are an utter fool, Selig!" she snapped. "Don't you see that this boy deliberately kicked Dmitri in order to goad you into doing something like this? Now we cannot question him further!"

Selig hung his head. "I am sorry, Lina."

She didn't answer him, but turned to the fat man, helped him to get up.

"Come, Dmitri," she said. "I'll help you into the office. Leave this brat here till he recovers. There is much to be done."

She aided him to arise and walked him, still groaning, to the door.

The chauffeur remained in the room with the unconscious boy.

"When he awakes," the woman said to the chauffeur from the threshold, "call us."

The fat man groaned, said through pain-twisted lips: "Yes. Call—me. I—will have something to—say to him!"

The chauffeur nodded, and watched them leave. Then he seated himself in the chair which Osman had vacated, and settled himself to wait for Tim Donovan to come to.*

CHAPTER 2
PRIDE BEFORE A FALL

WHILE TIM DONOVAN was being carried across town by the obese Dmitri Osman and the woman, Lina,

---

* AUTHOR'S NOTE: Readers of previous chronicles of the exploits of Operator 5 will already have recognized Tim Donovan as the irrepressible, freckle-faced Irish lad who has been Operator 5's constant companion through many dangers. On a rain-drenched night on New York's lower East Side, Tim Donovan once saved Operator 5 from an assassin's attack. Since then, the ace operative of the United States Intelligence Service and the freckle-faced boy have been almost inseparable. Operator 5 has trusted the lad with many a dangerous task that he might have hesitated to allot to a grown man. Due to Tim's youth, he cannot qualify as an Intelligence Agent. He therefore acts as Operator 5's unofficial assistant, and wears a ring with a secret mark which identifies him to Secret Service Agents everywhere. Readers will recall that in the last novel, "Rockets From Hell," it was Tim Donovan's ingenuity that finally broke the backbone of the monstrous plot of The Master against the United States.

James Christopher—Operator 5, ace of the United States Intelligence—was facing three men in a room on the third floor of the Custom House Building, on Bowling Green, in downtown New York.

The three men were seated. Operator 5 was standing, talking to them vehemently, urgently. As he spoke, he gestured toward a girl who stood beside him.

"Gentlemen," he was pleading, "you *must* believe what this young lady tells us. She is Katerina Saratoff, the sister of a very dear friend of mine, who died so that she might come here to give me the message. For two weeks I have tried to get you to listen to her. Today I practically forced my way in here. I beg of you, gentlemen, give this young lady five minutes of your time!"

One of the three men rose, glanced at the others, and cleared his throat. He was a tall man in his late fifties, and his bearing was distinguished, sedate. He was the Secretary of War—the man who had the last word on the disposition of the fighting forces of the United States. He adjusted his glasses on his thin, aquiline nose, and spoke sharply:

"Operator 5, you must realize that you are interfering with the embarkation of four thousand soldiers. The war in Europe—"

"The war in Europe be damned!" Jimmy Christopher broke in hotly. "Don't you realize, Mr. Secretary, that our own shores are in danger? What will you do when the enemy ships are sighted off our coastline?" He turned pleadingly to the two seated men. "You, General Falk, and you, Admiral Winston. Perhaps you will listen to me. This young lady has definite information that the Union of Asiatic States plans to attack the United States. You yourselves know that no news has come out of Asia for months. You know also, that Soviet Russia has been fighting desperately, fruitlessly, for her life on her eastern frontiers. You have heard rumors that a new dictator has sprung up in Asia, who has consolidated all the yellow races under a single banner. Yet—"

The man whom Jimmy Christopher had addressed as Admiral Winston raised a hand. He was a comparatively young man, in his early forties. He was attired in the full-dress uniform of a rear-admiral of the United States Navy. It was he who was to take command of the convoy sailing that evening—and who was scheduled to assume full charge of the Sanctioning Powers' Joint Fleet in Mediterranean waters.

He was smiling indulgently as he said:

"All these things may be quite true, Operator 5. But I should like to point out to you that even if there is a new dictator in Asia—even if the Asiatic States have conquered Russia—they can constitute no very serious menace to us. Our fleet has been brought up to full war-time capacity. We can literally blast any attacking force out of the ocean. Just what do you want us to do about this Asiatic attack that you fear so much?"

"This is no laughing matter, sir!" Jimmy said urgently. "Miss Saratoff here tells me that she and her brother covered eight hundred miles across Russia, in the wake of the retreating Soviet armies. She tells me that not a single pitched battle was fought, but that the Russian forces fell back constantly, leaving a clear path across Europe from Lake Baikal."

He turned to Katerina Saratoff, who bad been watching him breathlessly, and said, switching easily into Russian: "Let me have the message which Feodor wrote—quickly. Perhaps I can convince them now—"

He took the envelope which she extracted from her purse, and turned back to the three men, opening it and extracting the folded sheet of notepaper, covered with Russian hieroglyphics, written in pencil in a small, scholarly hand.

"This, gentlemen, is the letter which Feodor Saratoff wrote when he realized that he would never leave Russia alive. I won't take your time to translate and read it. But Saratoff hints here that the Dictator of the Union of Asiatic States has developed a new kind of warfare. He has advanced across Russia without fighting a single major engagement."

The tall man who had spoken first cleared his throat and stopped Jimmy Christopher. "No doubt these Asiatics bribed the craven Soviet commanders—"

JIMMY SHOOK his head. "There is more than bribery behind this, Mr. Secretary. There is some peculiar force which this coolie—who calls himself The Leopard—has developed and—"

28

JIMMY CHRISTOPHER

General Falk, the Chief of Staff of the United States, who had been sitting silent all this time, suddenly snapped his fingers in impatience, and exclaimed: "Bosh! Let this Leopard cross the Atlantic. We will show him—"

He stopped as a knock sounded on the door. "Come in!" he barked.

The door opened, and a young naval lieutenant entered, saluted briskly, and handed a dispatch to Admiral Winston.

"Captain Loring's compliments, sir," he said, with a manner of barely restrained excitement. "The radio room on the *Dakota* just picked up this message in code, from the Destroyer, *Macklin*. We tried to communicate with the *Macklin* at once after receiving it, sir, but were unable to raise them again."

Admiral Winston frowned, took the dispatch and glanced at the others. Then he unfolded it and his ruddy face grew pale as his eyes traveled over the typed words.

Suddenly he looked up, and his gaze met Jimmy Christopher's.

"Operator 5," he said in a strangely altered voice, "it appears that part of what you have been telling us has come true!"

There were gasps of astonishment from the Secretary of War and from General Falk. Winston motioned them to silence, and read aloud from the dispatch:

HAVE SIGHTED FLEET OF FORTY SHIPS THIR-TY-EIGHT DEGREES NORTH LAT SEVENTY DEGREES EAST LONG CANNOT ASCERTAIN NATION FOR THEY ARE FLYING BLACK FLAG WITH FIGURE OF RED LEOPARD HAVE COUNTED THIRTY CONVOYS AND TEN SHIPS OF WAR STANDING BY FOR ORDERS
JOHN DENNY

COMMANDER
DESTROYER MACKLIN

For a moment there was startled silence in the room. From outside came the blare of trumpets and the roll of drums as marching men debouched from Broadway onto the docks and prepared to embark.

The Secretary of War snatched the sheet from Winston's hand, reread it himself, handed it to Falk.

Jimmy Christopher whispered in Katerina Saratoff's ear a translation of the message, and her dark eyes suddenly snapped fire.

She said in Russian to Jimmy:

"It is the Leopard! I shall pray now, every moment, that the Holy Virgin give you strength and wit and courage to avenge the death of my brother!"

Jimmy said to her somberly: "If my guess is right, Katerina, it will take more than prayer to lick this Leopard. From Feodor's letter, I should judge that we are going to be invaded within twenty-four hours!"

He turned from the girl to hear Admiral Winston say to the Secretary of War:

"This Leopard is in for a huge surprise. I ask you, sir, to give me full command of the Atlantic Fleet. The troopships will have to wait for their convoys. There are more than a hundred warships along the Atlantic seaboard, and I can have most of them here within a few hours. I will go meet this Leopard, and blow him to Kingdom Come!"

"You have full authority, Winston," the Secretary said without hesitation. "The fleet is yours!"

WINSTON BEAMED with satisfaction, snatched up the telephone on the desk, and began to snap instructions. Jimmy Christopher approached the Secretary, said low-voiced:

"There is another matter, sir, that I must call to your attention." There was no trace of elation, of the I-told-you-so attitude in Jimmy's manner. These men had laughed at him only a moment ago, and his prediction and warning had come true, dramatically. Yet he refrained from calling it to the Secretary's attention.

"In Feodor Saratoff's note, here, he warns me that the Leopard has placed agents of his in key positions with our armed forces, as well as with the large industrial plants throughout the country. Perhaps—"

The Secretary put a kindly hand on his shoulder. "Do not concern yourself about that, Operator 5. Within a few hours, this Leopard will have become a thing of the past. With ten warships, he cannot hope to oppose our splendid fleet. Either he will turn tail and head back to Asia, or he will be annihilated."

"That may be so, sir," Jimmy Christopher insisted stubbornly. "But it might be well to make some preparations to receive him in the event that he manages to break through our fleet. The four thousand men who are embarking now are about the only effective armed forces in the East. The training camps have only raw youths—"

The Secretary laughed. "You are far too pessimistic, Operator 5. The Leopard will never break through."

Jimmy was about to protest further, but at that moment Winston put down the telephone, turned from the desk, his face beaming with excitement.

"Everything is arranged!" he exclaimed. "Within three hours every available squadron will be ready for action. We will teach the Leopard a lesson that he won't soon forget. I am ordering the embarkation to continue. As soon as we have disposed of those tubs from Asia, I will sail for Europe as originally planned!"

Jimmy Christopher frowned. "Why not keep those men here, Admiral? You can return after the engagement, and go on with the embarkation. It's little enough protection for New York if anything should happen to the fleet. And you must remember that the Leopard controls some peculiar instrument of warfare—"

"Bah!" The admiral snapped his fingers. "Those Soviet soldiers were nothing but rank cowards; and their officers were probably bribed. I'll concede that your information about the Leopard's arrival was correct—but even then, it's nothing to get worried about. It's ridiculous to think that ten battleships and thirty tubs full of yellow soldiers could constitute a serious threat to America!"

The Secretary of War was nodding in agreement with the naval officer. "Your zeal is commendable, Operator 5. But I think that you may well leave the handling of this business to Admiral Winston from now on."

Hopelessly, Jimmy Christopher turned away from them, took Katerina Saratoff by the arm. There was no use arguing with these men. As he led the girl out of the room, none of them paid him any attention.

33

Outside, Katerina said to him: "I am afraid, Operator 5—afraid for your country. Those men are fools. They do not understand that the Leopard would not come against them were he not sure of victory. The Leopard knows how strong your fleet is; and he is not a fool. He has some plan to destroy it—I am sure!"

Jimmy shrugged. "What can I do, Katerina? Those men hold the country's fate in their hands. They are the highest officers in the land; I am only a number in the Intelligence Service!"

CHAPTER 3
THE MAN BREAKER

LESS THAN two hundred miles from the coast of New England, the great Atlantic Fleet of the United States was steaming eastward.

The long, lean, metal monsters cut through the clear blue water, holding formations, squadron by squadron. Above them, and far ahead, roared the naval aircraft, while from the stern of the Dakota, the huge new flagship of the fleet, there fluttered the two-starred pennant of Rear-Admiral Stanley Winston.

A hundred and nine ships comprised that mighty fleet. There were five capital ships of the line, besides the Dakota; there were sixty-four destroyers, eleven heavy cruisers, the aircraft carriers, Langley and Mattson, four submarine tenders, and twenty-two submarines. Nine squadron pennants billowed in the wind.

Behind the fleet lagged supply and hospital ships.

Inter-squadron and inter-division messages crackled over

wireless sets, and intra-division signal flags slid up and down on signal-hoists.

On every ship the men were all at battle stations, and decks were cleared for action. Grim, tight-lipped officers waited word for the reconnoitering planes that the enemy had been sighted.

In a cabin on the flagship, Dakota, Admiral Stanley Winston sat before a desk piled with memorandum, lists and charts. Though he hadn't slept the night before, his uniform was spotless, and the two silver stars and foul anchor of his shoulder insignia gleamed with bright newness.

His voice crackled as he issued swift orders which sent junior officers scurrying to the wireless room with messages for the fleet. At his elbow stood Lieutenant Earl Ward, the Admiral's personal secretary. On the desk was an ashtray littered with dead butts of cigarettes. As soon as Winston finished one, Lieutenant Ward would hand him another, light it for him. It was a standing matter of knowledge in the navy that Winston, brilliant sea strategist that he was, would be lost without Ward to attend to the little details of his personal comfort, which Winston himself utterly forgot when in action.

Now, Lieutenant Ward bent over his superior, whispered: "How about a little rest, sir? It may be a matter of hours before we contact the enemy. You've got everything in hand. You haven't slept—"

Winston waved him aside impatiently. "I'll sleep after the engagement—if there is any, Ward. There are still things to be done." His voice assumed an edge of irritation. "I have to receive this young fool that Intelligence is sending out. I don't know why in God's name they should send me an Intelligence man at this time. He'll probably get under our feet and clog up the works. Those fellows think they've got a monopoly of brains!"

He picked up the phone at his elbow, barked: "Give me the bridge!" Then when he got his connection: "My compliments to Captain Loring, and instruct him to watch for an autogyro that should be approaching us about this time. He is to signal it to alight on the Langley. Its occupant is to be brought to me at once!"

He hung up, sat back in the swivel chair, and looked up at his orderly with an air of utter weariness. They were alone in the cabin for the first time that morning. Suddenly his stern face broke into a warm smile. He reached up and patted Ward on the shoulder.

"Relax, Lieutenant," he said. "You seem to be all on edge. Why the worry? This Leopard from Asia may be a big shot on land, but I'll warrant you he's never met a fleet like this. We'll blow him out of the water. There won't be a trace of his forty ships an hour after we sight them!"

Lieutenant Ward fidgeted nervously, his glance straying through the porthole, through which he could catch a glimpse of a long line of destroyers that steamed to leeward of them. "It isn't that, sir," he said uneasily.

"It's you I'm worried about. You haven't taken a minute's rest in the last forty-eight hours. Perhaps a little coffee—?"

"Good idea!" Winston grunted. He glanced at a small electric stove in the corner. "I see you've got some brewing. Let's have a cup."

WARD NODDED, and went to the stove. An ensign entered, and saluted. "Captain Loring's respects, sir. The plane you are expecting has been sighted, flying very high. It should land within a few minutes."

"All right," the admiral growled. "Have him brought right over."

The ensign left, and Ward brought over a cup of black coffee, which he placed on the desk.

"Have some yourself, Ward," the admiral said in kindly fashion. "You can use it."

"No thanks, sir. I've had too much of it already."

Winston sipped the hot black liquid. "What do you think of that, Ward?" he grumbled. "Intelligence is going to teach us how to fight a sea battle. It's that Operator 5, I suppose. He tried to sell Falk and myself some damned silly bill of goods this morning, and now he must have got to the Secretary's ear again, and convinced him. His story is that the Leopard will lick us by making a couple of passes in the air, and saying some magic hocus-pocus! Intelligence! Bah!"

He set the cup down with a bang, and arose to pace impatiently up and down the cabin.

Ward stood aside respectfully as the admiral pushed past him, and stared out of the porthole. The speeding vessel rocked

OPERATOR 5

hardly at all as it ate up the knots. Streaming far out behind it, in a huge V on either side, churned squadron after squadron of the most powerful sea-fighting machine in the world.

Almost subconsciously, Winston's shoulders straightened, and the weariness which he had felt fell from him as a discarded mantle. Pride shone in his eyes.

"Do you know, Ward," he said over his shoulder, "it's a queer feeling—having all these ships under my orders. Imagine! I have supreme command over a hundred and nine fighting vessels. This whole fleet moves only at my word, stops only at my word! When I was a cub at Annapolis, I never dreamed that such power would one day lie in my hands!"

"It's a great responsibility, sir," Ward said quietly behind him. "I'd be afraid—"

He stopped as a knock sounded on the door. An ensign entered, saluted. "Captain Loring's respects, sir. Our planes have sighted the enemy fleet, sir!"

Winston's eyes gleamed. He finished the rest of the coffee at a gulp, and arose. "My compliments to Captain Loring. Tell him that I will be on the bridge in ten minutes. In the mean-time, have the gun crews of every ship get the range from the planes—"

The ensign interrupted. "Captain Loring instructed me to tell you, sir, that our planes are acting strangely. They have ceased to communicate with us by radio, and they are veering about erratically. Captain Loring respectfully requests that you come up at once, sir. He is afraid there is something radically wrong!"

For a moment there was silence in the cabin, while Winston's

38

suddenly haggard eyes met the glance of Lieutenant Ward. There was suddenly a queer sort of lassitude in the Admiral's eyes, that had not been there a few moments before, even in spite of his utter physical exhaustion. Almost blindly he stumbled out of the door of the cabin.

"Strange, very strange," he was muttering as he walked unsteadily along the companionway, with the lieutenant and the ensign trailing him. "Very strange...."

CHAPTER 4
THE FINGER OF DOOM

WHEN OPERATOR 5 left the Custom House Building with Katerina Saratoff, he did not take her out through the front way. At a little-used side entrance a high-powered convertible coupé was parked. The top was up. The glass sides had also been raised, making it in effect, a coupé. No one could have suspected that the canvas top really covered sheet steel, or that the innocent appearing sides and hood of the car were of bullet-proof construction, with bullet-proof glass in the windows. The car was a veritable moving fortress.

At the wheel sat a young, chestnut-haired girl whose softly-modeled face and shining eyes formed a distinct contrast to the reserved, patrician features of Katerina Saratoff. This girl was Diane Elliot, star reporter for the Amalgamated Press. She was one of the few people with whom Operator 5 was closely associated; and she was, by the same token, one of the very few who knew that the person listed on the rolls of the Secret Service only by the designation of Operator 5 was really a human being, with emotions and feelings like other people.

She opened the door of the car hastily now, as Operator 5 and Katerina Saratoff appeared, and moved over to make room for them in the wide seat.

The Secret Service ace took the wheel, guided the car expertly away from the curb, and headed uptown, glancing backward several times to make sure they were not followed.

It was only after they were well away from the Custom House that Diane Elliot spoke. Her bright blue eyes were clouded with worry.

"Jimmy! Didn't you say that Tim Donovan was to meet us here?"

He nodded, gazing ahead as he threaded his way skillfully through the cluttered traffic of Fulton Street. He was avoiding Broadway because of the marching troops, and the narrow street was crowded with vehicles which had been shunted here by the police.

"Yes," he said. "I told Tim to come down here. I wanted him to keep a lookout in case we were observed. The Leopard has a lot of agents in New York, and they're darned anxious to get their hands on Katerina." He glanced sideways at the Russian girl, who was sitting between Diane and himself, saw her shudder at the mention of the Leopard. He smiled grimly. "It seems that the big coolie from Asia has taken a fancy to Katerina. I'm sure she appreciates the compliment!"

Diane exclaimed hurriedly: "But about Tim, Jimmy! I looked for him. He wasn't anywhere around."

Jimmy Christopher shrugged. "Maybe he was tied up at the house, with dad. We'll probably find him home—"

"No, no, Jimmy!" Diane's voice throbbed with anxiety. "I phoned home a little while ago, and there was no answer. I'm afraid—something's—happened! Your dad should have answered the phone. He said he'd wait for us to come back—"

Operator 5's face was suddenly bleak. His father, John Christopher, who had been Q-6 in the Intelligence Service until forced into semi-retirement by a wound received in the discharge of his duty, presided over the brownstone house in the middle forties where Jimmy Christopher made his home while in New York. Between the father and son there existed a remarkable mutual understanding and love.

Jimmy Christopher frowned at the news Diane had just given him. "It's not like Dad to leave the phone unattended at a time like this. I wonder—?"

HIS LIPS clamped tight in a thin, grim line. His foot pushed down on the accelerator and he made the long roadster squirm through traffic with an exhibition of almost unbelievable driving skill, until he had fought free of the snarl of cars around Brooklyn Bridge. Then he raced north up Lafayette Street.

Katerina Saratoff put a sympathetic hand on his arm. "You—fear that something has happened to your father, Operator 5?"

· TIM DONOVAN ·

"I don't know," he muttered. "Tim should have been down here. If he isn't, and if Dad doesn't answer the phone—"

Diane, in an effort to take his mind from thoughts of Q-6's possible danger, asked: "How did you make out with the Secretary of War and with Admiral Winston, Jimmy?"

"We didn't make out at all, Di! While I was warning them about the Leopard, they got word that his fleet had been sighted out at sea. That should have proved to them that I know what I was talking about—that there was some truth to Feodor's claim that the Leopard has some strange power. But no—they're sending out the whole Atlantic Fleet under Winston to meet them. I tried to get them to hold these troops in New York, in case the fleet should be beaten, but they couldn't see it. In a couple of hours, Admiral Winston will take out the whole sea power of the United States—and they may be destroyed, just the way the Leopard destroyed the Soviet resistance!"

"And there's nothing you can do about it?"

"Nothing! They won't listen to us. Will they, Katerina?"

The Russian girl's face was white. "God forgive them," she said, very slow, "for they know not what they do! They are delivering their country to the claws of the Leopard!"

They drove in silence until they reached the brownstone house which was recorded in the files of Intelligence as "Address Y," and which was the home of John Christopher.

Operator 5 did not stop at the door. He drove slowly past glancing keenly at the building, and up and down the street. At the far corner, satisfied that no one was watching the place, he

made a U turn, and pulled up before the door. Quickly, he and the two girls got out of the car and entered the house.

Just inside the hallway he stopped short, his blood suddenly cold as he gazed down at the pitiful body on the floor. Diane and Katerina pressed close behind him, and Diane uttered a choked cry.

Jimmy Christopher knelt swiftly beside the body, gasped in a broken voice: "Dad!"

The man who lay face up on the floor was like an old edition of Operator 5. The cleanly-etched features, the wide forehead, the straight nose. The hair, though, was not dark, but gray. And the eyes were closed, while the head rested in a great pool of blood from a wound behind the left ear.

Jimmy Christopher bent low, raised his father's head gently. His lips were a tight, straight line as he placed his cheek against the unconscious man's lips, waited for a warm breath that would tell him there was still life in that body. The agony in his eyes was hidden from the two girls behind him.

Diane came around opposite him in the hallway, and knelt on the other side of the unconscious Q-6. She said huskily: "No—wonder he—didn't answer the phone! Jimmy! Is he—dead?"

Operator 5 raised his head, his eyes gleaming with hope. "No, Di! Quick! On the phone, and get Doctor Harlan!"

She nodded, got to her feet, and hurried down the hall into a room at the right.

Jimmy Christopher raised the body of his father tenderly in his arms, carried him up the stairs into a bedroom. Katerina Saratoff followed, hurriedly prepared the bed, then bustled about the room in search of water, towels, antiseptic.

When Jimmy would have helped her she pushed him aside. "I know what to do," she whispered. "I nursed many men in Russia!"

Jimmy knelt beside the bed, his eyes fastened to the pallid face of his father. The pillow was rapidly becoming stained with blood.

KATERINA CAME back with the things she had found, gently pushed Jimmy out of the way, and her cool white hands flew with the efficient speed of a ministering angel. Diane came into the room, and at a questioning glance from Jimmy, she nodded, then hurried over to help Katerina.

The wound in the back of John Christopher's head was an ugly one, evidently made with some blunt weapon. Matted hair and broken skin clotted it, and Katerina swabbed it out.

Q-6 stirred, groaned at the pain, and his eyelids fluttered open. Diane exclaimed: "Dad! Thank God! Lie still, Dad. Don't move!"

But John Christopher stubbornly kept his eyes open, muttered weakly: "Jimmy! They got—Tim! Must—" He groaned again, closed his eyes, then started to mumble once more.

Jimmy bent over him, said anxiously: "Keep quiet, Dad. You—"

He stopped as his father's voice came to him once more, faintly. "They—broke in… fat man and—pock-marked man. Got—Tim. I—fought—with them… got—fat man's—fingerprints!"

"Where, Dad?" Jimmy asked eagerly.

"Here… on wristwatch strap… go get 'em, Jimmy!" And John Christopher's gray head fell back on Katerina's tenderly supporting arm.

For a moment, Jimmy held his breath, thinking his father was dead. But a sigh of relief escaped him as he noted the slow rise and fall of John Christopher's chest. He leaned over, and lifted his father's wrist, carefully unbuckled the silver chain of the wrist watch.

His eager eyes examined its surface, detected the unmistakable smudges of two prints—a thumb and another finger.

"Good old Dad!" he exclaimed. "He must have struggled with one of them, just to get those prints!"

Diane looked up from the bedside. "Jimmy! What are you going to do? Tim—"

"I'm going to find him!" Operator 5 said harshly. "And find the ones who did that to Dad! Stay here, Di, with Katerina. I'll call back to find out how he is!"

And without looking back, he hurried out of the room, and downstairs to the car. Outside, he met Doctor Harlan, who was the unofficial surgeon to the men of the Intelligence Service. He gripped Harlan's arm.

"Doc! It's dad! They got him in the head." His lips twitched. "I've—got to go, Doc. You'll do your best—more than your best?"

Doctor Harlan nodded warmly. "You know I will, Jimmy. Go ahead with your work—and leave your father to me."

Jimmy tore himself away, got into the car and drove downtown, to police headquarters. Paralleling his course, only a block away, festive men and women were shouting in acclaim, showering marching troops with confetti, cheering them on toward their embarkation. Out on the Hudson, giant ships were steaming down toward the Bay to meet other ships, summoned from along the Atlantic seaboard, to go out and meet an approaching enemy. None knew of the tragedy in the brownstone house. There was none to share Jimmy Christopher's anxiety with him—anxiety about his father, about Tim, and about the coming naval engagement.

At police headquarters, Operator 5 showed credentials indicating that he was one, George Weakly, of the Department of Justice. He asked to have the prints on the watch band checked at once.

HE WAITED, fiercely restraining his impatience and anxiety. It was a very slim chance—the chance that the man who had struck his father would have a criminal record, would have his prints filed here. He thought, as he paced up and down the little anteroom where he waited, that it would be a grisly irony if his father's sacrifice in fighting that man were to go for naught.

But in less than five minutes, a grinning fingerprint man came into the room with a card and photographs. "Here's your man, Wakely! How's that for cooperation?"

Jimmy seized the card and the pictures. The name typed at the top of the card brought recollections to him:

OSMAN, DMITRI, *alias* Michael Feene, *alias* Franz Broca.
5 ft. 8 in., wt. 192 lbs. Hair brownish, sparse: eyes grayish brown.

Arrested, March 15, 1919—suspicion of murder—discharged, lack of evidence.

Arrested, May 21, 1922—homicide—acquitted, Gen'l Sessions.

Arrested, May 9, 1927—for extradition at request of Surete Generale, Paris. Wanted for espionage. Turned over to U.S. Marshal for hearing on extradition request. Discharged by U.S. Comm'r. Hendricks—charge not extraditable.

No convictions.

Present occupation: Proprietor of Dance Studio. 720 West 103 St (Note: Seems to be legitimate; precinct house notified to keep under surveillance, reports he has numerous pupils among foreign-born.)

There was more, but Jimmy skipped it. He fastened his eyes on the picture of the oily, fat Dmitri Osman, committed every feature to his memory. Then he returned them, together with the card, to the fingerprint man, uttered hasty thanks, and hurried out. Downstairs, in the lobby, he entered a telephone booth, dialed a number.

"Operator 5, talking!" he snapped. "Give me Z-7, quick!" When he got the connection he spoke crisply, concisely: "Chief! Dad's been—"

"I know," broke in Z-7, the head of the United States Intelligence Service, who was almost a second father to Jimmy Christopher. His voice was full of sympathy. "I've been trying to get you, and I phoned Address Y. Diane told me about your dad, and about Tim. What in the world would they want to kidnap Tim for?"

"I think I know, Chief. They want to make Tim talk. They want to find out where Katerina Saratoff is. They're agents of the Leopard, or I miss my guess. And Chief—you remember Dmitri Osman, the international spy? He's in this. Dad got his prints on his wristwatch strap. And I've got Osman's address. They may have Tim there—trying to make him talk. Give me a couple of men, Chief. I'm going to raid that place."

"You'll have 'em, Jimmy. You'll have more than a couple. I'll send you a dozen! What's the address?"

Jimmy Christopher gave it then hung up. He phoned his father's house, learned that Doctor Harlan was having Q-6 moved to a hospital.

"Is it that bad, Di?" he asked hoarsely. "Will he—"

Diane Elliot's voice was husky, tired. "The doctor doesn't know yet, Jimmy. They—they'll know by morning. Katerina and I are going with him to the hospital. We've got special permission. What about Tim, Jimmy?"

"I think I know where they've got him. I'm raiding the place. I'll call you later." He got the name of the hospital, hung up, and went out once more to the car, raced uptown to meet the raiding squad....

CHAPTER 5
TREASON TRAIL

TIM DONOVAN groaned, stirred, and blinked. Then he opened his eyes. He closed them again at once, because fiery, shooting pains were stabbing through his head. His mouth was parched, and his throat was dry. For a moment he thought he was at home, awakening from some sort of nightmare. Slowly, recollection struggled back through the dreadful throbbing behind his temples.

He opened his eyes once more, and the room swam around; the walls performed grotesque antics about him, and the ceiling seemed to be tipping drunkenly. He turned painfully from his back to his side, and put a hand gingerly to the lump on the back of his head.

His gaze met the stolid glance of the pockmarked man, Selig, who sat watching him, with a gun on his knee. The man's figure seemed blurred, and his face looked like a gruesome gargoyle that advanced and receded, grew bigger and smaller, and danced around.

Tim managed a rueful smile, and said: "Hello, Funny-face. That was an awful sock you handed me. Hope to return the compliment some time."

The other snarled, and rose from his chair, went to the door and opened it. He called down the corridor, and the white-coated Chinese who had admitted them came, peered in, nodded, and padded away. In a few moments footsteps sounded, and the woman, Lina, appeared, followed by Dmitri Osman.

The fat man waddled in, his small eyes fixed intently, viciously on Tim. He said nothing, but came up to the cot and seized the boy's left arm in both of his big fat hands, twisted it cruelly. Tim gasped with the sudden agony, and his face went white with pain. His head swam. He felt the bone of his arm was about to be torn from its socket.

But the woman, Lina, cried out: "Osman! You fool! He'll faint again. We must question him first. Later you can pay him for the kick in the stomach!"

Osman growled deep in his throat, like an angry animal. But under the whiplash of the woman's voice, he released Tim's arm.

The boy lay panting on the cot, weak with agony.

Osman stepped back from him, deliberately twisted his face into a grimace that was meant to be a suave smile. His little eyes burned with malice. "All right, Lina," he said. "I—wait!"

The woman turned to Tim Donovan, and she too, smiled, her red lips curving into soft lines, and her eyes suddenly seeming to caress the boy.

"My poor lad," she said. "You see, this man is so very hard to keep in leash. He wants to do so dreadful things to you. Why do you not speak, and spare yourself suffering? Tell us what you know of Katerina Saratoff. You are in the confidence of Operator 5. You know where he hides her. Speak, and I promise that you shall go unharmed."

Tim's head still throbbed mercilessly; his shoulder muscles still ached, with a dull, twisted pain. Yet he grinned up at her impudently.

"Believe me, lady," he said, exerting a tremendous effort to keep his voice steady, "Fatty is going to get his when Operator 5 catches up with him. You can't get away—"

He stopped as Lina raised a long, white hand. "Foolish boy! In a few hours, your Operator 5 will be as helpless as the rest of your country. From Asia comes the Leopard. Soon he will march into New York. The fools go out to meet him in stately

The fat man's automatic exploded as Jimmy leaped in!

ships; their ships will turn tail and run. The Leopard will land with his conquering might. For no man can resist the Leopard!"

She spoke with such earnestness, with such intensity of feeling, that Tim forgot his pain. He raised himself on an elbow, asked her: "Then why are you so anxious to find Katerina Saratoff? If you're so sure the Leopard will be top hand, why don't you wait?"

The woman cast a side glance at Osman, and at the chauffeur, Selig. She shrugged. "We are only servants of the Leopard. The Leopard orders, and we obey. He has sworn that his first stroke on setting foot in the United States, shall be to punish Katerina Saratoff for defying him in Russia. He wishes her to be presented to him when be lands."

She came closer to the cot, said urgently: "Speak, boy! I have told you all you need to know. Now you must talk, or else I cannot help you."

Tim glared up at her. "Lady," he said, "if you were a man, I'd tell you to go to hell. Being that you're not a man, I'm only thinking it!"

Lina's face was suddenly convulsed with frustrated rage. She swung away from him to Osman. "He is yours, Dmitri!" she blazed. "Do with him what you like!"

OSMAN'S THICK lips parted in a smile of vicious satisfaction. His thick hands clasped and unclasped, as if they already had the boy in their grip. "Now," he gloated, "you will see—"

He ceased talking as the sound of a smashing window came to them from somewhere in the house. It was followed at once by another crash of breaking glass, and by a shout in the high-

53

pitched voice of the Chinese servant. There was a revolver shot out in the hall; which mingled with the quick, short barks of an automatic.

Osman was fat, but he was a man of action. He swung away from Tim's cot, and an automatic appeared in his hand. He ripped open the door, launched himself into the hall, followed by Selig, who had also drawn a gun.

The woman, Lina, stood with blanched cheeks, one hand at her breast. From where he lay, propped once more on his elbow, Tim could see into the hallway, could see Osman crouching, and firing toward the front of the house, and Selig beside him.

The room, and the hall outside were filled with the thunderous reverberations of gunfire, and with the acrid fumes of smoke, which stung Tim's nostrils. From the front of the house he could see flash after flash from the guns of the attackers. Slugs ricocheted into the room. Selig uttered a strangled cry, pitched backward, writhed on the floor, and then lay still, almost at Lina's feet.

The woman snapped out of her momentary fright and shouted: "Osman! Back! Back in here!"

The fat man heard her above the gun roar, and sprang back into the room, still shooting.

"The boy!" Lina shouted. "Use him as a shield!"

Osman fired the last shot from his automatic kicked the door shut, and his fat fingers raced as he inserted another clip. A heavy body thudded against the door, and Osman, his teeth showing in a wolfish grin, stepped back, seized Tim by the collar, and dragged him upright, held him in front of himself.

Lina had stooped and picked up the heavy revolver which Selig had dropped.

For a moment, the shots ceased coming from outside, and a cautious hand tried the knob of the door. Osman called out: "We have the boy here. If you shoot, you will kill him!"

Tim Donovan was struggling like a wildcat in the grip of the fat man, striving to twist around so that his fists could reach his captor's face. He shouted: "Come in shooting, Jimmy! To hell with him!"

Osman swore under his breath, raised the barrel of the automatic to strike at Tim's head. But just then a terrific jolt jarred the door, and it creaked on its frame. Osman stepped back involuntarily, swung his automatic down to fire through the wood.

A shot sounded from outside, and the lock flew loose, the wood around it splintered and smoking. The door swung open, and a man came charging in, gun raised to fire. The man was Operator 5, and behind were other Secret Service men. Jimmy Christopher saw Tim in the grip of Osman, shielding the fat man, and he held his finger away from the trigger of his gun, pulling up short.

Osman's lips were foaming at the edges. He kept his grip on Tim, raised the automatic so that its muzzle pointed at Operator 5. His finger contracted....

And Tim Donovan, exerting every last ounce of strength in his pain-wracked body, twisted, pushed out with both hands, and shoved Osman's gun arm far to the right. The fat man's automatic exploded, the slug going wild into the wall.

In that second, Jimmy Christopher leaped in, switched

his gun from right hand to left, and
brought it down hard on Osman's
temple. Osman's eyes rolled up, the
automatic dropped from nerveless
fingers, and his grip on Tim relaxed.
Slowly his body collapsed to the floor.

Lina had clicked the trigger of the
revolver she had picked up from the
floor, aiming at Operator 5, but Selig
must have emptied before he was hit. For the hammer fell on an
empty chamber, and before she could move, other Secret Service
men had swarmed into the room to overpower her.

Tim Donovan was wobbling on his feet, and Operator 5
gripped him, demanded anxiously: "Tim! You all in one piece?"

The boy took a grip on himself, and grinned. "I'm okay. I'm
a little frayed here and there, but I guess I'll last." Suddenly his
tone changed, became somber. "How's dad, Jimmy? Is he—?"

"Dad's in the hospital," Jimmy told him shortly. "I've got to
call up to find out how he is. Who—?"

Tim's eyes dropped to Osman, who was slowly getting to his
feet. "This guy socked him, Jimmy."

OPERATOR 5'S eyes were bleak as be turned to the other
Secret Service men in the room. "Will you boys leave for a few
minutes?" He asked softly. "I've got a little business with this
gentleman!"

The men glanced at each other knowingly, winked at Jimmy,
and filed out. Two of them, holding the woman captive, led
her to the door. As she passed Jimmy she stopped, let her eyes

wander over his trim, well-knit figure. Then she looked up into his face.

"So you are the famous Operator 5?" she queried. "You are clever, to have found this place so quickly. You and I, perhaps, can do some business, too. When you are through with that swine—" her glance flicked to Osman—"come and talk to me."

Operator 5 did not answer. His eyes were cold, hard, and he did not take them from the fat man. His body was held taut.

The woman shrugged, allowed herself to be led out. Tim remained in the room. He picked up Osman's automatic, went and took a position with his back to the door.

"Go ahead, Jimmy," he said, very low. "Give it to him!"

Osman regarded Operator 5 out of his narrow slits of eyes. There was a trace of fear in them. "What are you going to do?" he asked.

Jimmy Christopher's thinned lips moved with cold precision as he said: "The man whom you wounded back at the house is my father. He is at the hospital now, dying. I am going to put my hands around your throat and choke you to death!"

Osman's teeth bared in a snarl. He crouched, his two hands hanging low.

Jimmy Christopher stepped in, and Osman suddenly lifted both hands, fingers held stiffly forward, and poked at Jimmy's eyes.

But Operator 5 had learned that trick many years ago in Constantinople. His head flicked back out of reach; and at the same time, he brought up his own hands, caught Osman's two forefingers, and pushed forward and down.

There were two short, ugly snaps of cracking bone, and Osman's face drained of color. He uttered a short, whimpering cry, staggered backward, and raised his hands stupidly, looked at the dangling forefingers. They were both broken.

Jimmy said softly: "That's for what you did to Tim, Mr. Osman. I'm not blind. I can see that you've been torturing the kid. I'm not through, either. I've got a few more little tricks to show you before I kill you!"

He came slowly closer to the fat man, like an inevitable nemesis.

Osman cringed away from him, all the fight gone out of his fat body. "For the love of God," he whimpered, "be merciful! I cannot stand pain; I will do whatever you want. But do not hurt me!"

Jimmy Christopher's lips curled in scorn. "You can dish it out, but you can't take it, eh? Well, you've got to take it. Or—" his voice lowered—"would you prefer to tell me a few things?"

"Anything! Anything!" Osman gasped. There were lines of sweat running down his round face.

"All right. Tell me how the Leopard plans to win America."

"I do not know that. I swear I do not know! We, here, are not in the Leopard's confidence. *Wait!*" As Jimmy came closer, his voice rose to a screech, and the words tumbled from his quivering lips. "I only know that the Leopard can make armies to retreat before him, and can melt all defense. I do not know how. But I can tell you that he has agents planted with the fleet. Those agents will see that the fleet is destroyed."

"Their names?" Operator 5's voice crackled. "Quick!"

Osman fumbled in his pocket, drew out a folded slip of paper. "Lina and I enlisted them all. But we do not know their duties. We handed them sealed instructions which were mailed to us."

His shaking hand extended the paper to Jimmy, who took it, stepped back, and ran his eye down the list of six names. He whistled. "No wonder the Leopard is so confident!" he exclaimed to Tim. "These are all executive officers!"

Tim suggested: "Call up Admiral Winston, Jimmy, and have him hold those men on shore—"

"Too late, Tim. The fleet has sailed. Here's the wireless operator on the *Dakota*, on the list. We'd never be able to get a message through to Winston. And here's Lieutenant Ward, Winston's personal secretary."

Suddenly he went to the door, pulled it open. "All right, boys," he called to the other Secret Service men. "You can come in."

He turned Osman over into their custody, watched them leave with the fat man, and the woman, Lina, who kept looking back at him all the time, but who said nothing. Jimmy knew that she guessed Osman had talked.

As soon as the men were gone, leaving two of their number on guard in the house, Operator 5 swung to Tim Donovan. "How do you feel, kid? Equal to a little flight?"

Tim flexed his muscles. "As good as ever, Jimmy. Where do we go this time?"

"We're going to use my autogyro. We're flying out to the fleet, and have a personal interview with Admiral Winston. God grant that we get there before he sights the Leopard!"

CHAPTER 6
DISASTER AT SEA!

T HE WIDE stretch of the Atlantic Ocean was dotted with little specks from which thin streams of smoke rose in wavering spirals.

To the two figures in the autogyro high up near the clouds, the panorama was vast, the ships merely tiny shells whose decks seemed to swarm with insects.

Those insects were United States marines, hurrying to battle stations. From their vantage point, high above the planes of the fleet, the mighty formation of the United States Navy appeared strangely picayune to Operator 5 and to Tim Donovan.

Operator 5 was piloting and Tim was scanning the ocean beyond the fleet with a pair of binocular telescopes. The thought occurred to Jimmy Christopher that it was thus with everything that man did—down on the earth, it all seemed so important—his father dying in a hospital, with Diane and Katerina at his bedside; Winston, confident in the vast floating armament which he commanded; the Leopard, seeking world dominion while Europe writhed in the death-throes of war. They loomed so large down below, while up here they receded to minute proportions. Jimmy wondered how all those things must look to God.

He snapped out of his reverie as Tim's arm rose and fell over the side of the cockpit, pointing to a cluster of smoke spirals far to the east of the fleet. Jimmy picked up his own binocular telescopes, leveled them down at the spot indicated. The powerful glasses brought everything up close to his eyes, and he discerned a small flotilla, steaming in close formation directly for the United States Fleet! At the masthead of each of those ships he made out the peculiar ensign with the figure of the crouching leopard.

He spoke into the instrument connecting with Tim's earphones. "The Leopard's got something up his sleeve, Tim, or he'd never sail so boldly for a fleet more than twice his size. And we're too late. There goes the first gun."

A puff of smoke had billowed out from a foreword gun on the *Dakota*, and as if at a signal, the long V of the American ships spread out into a straight line.

It was then that Jimmy Christopher observed the peculiar actions of the United States planes. They were veering about, flying in odd directions, as if the pilots did not know exactly what to do, or where to go. Suddenly they turned, streaked back for their mother ships, the *Langley* and the *Mattson*. The first plane to reach the *Langley* bumped and bounced in an awkward landing, crashed its gear. The pilot of the second plane had not waited to see if the runway was clear, and he thundered down to end in a smashing holocaust, tangled with the first. Almost the same thing happened on the *Mattson*. In a moment, both aircraft carriers were a mass of living flame, and the other planes circled helplessly around them, unable to land, apparently at a loss as to what to do.

Jimmy Christopher watched, his eyes clouded with dread. "*Tim!*" he gasped into the transmitter. "They're without orders! Something's happened on the *Dakota!*"

Indeed, the flagship was steaming in an aimless circle, while the other ships of the line slowed their speed, also began to wander aimlessly. A destroyer rammed a heavy cruiser, and a huge pillar of flame erupted into the air. Smoke and fire engulfed the two ships, and when the wind blew it away, there was little left of them but the stern of the cruiser, rearing up into the air. Both ships had sunk in less than five minutes. Other ships rammed each other now, and soon the whole fleet was entangled in a snarl of aimlessly wandering, unguided ships. Many of the planes streaked down into the water, apparently out of control.

Half of the great fleet which had sailed so majestically only a few minutes before was now nothing but a helpless mass of wreckage; while the other half, including the *Dakota*, turned tail and ran.

And behind them steamed the forty ships of the Leopard, proudly victorious in their first battle with the greatest fleet in the Atlantic—victorious in a battle in which they had not struck a single blow!

JIMMY CHRISTOPHER circled the scene of wreckage and death, grinding his teeth helplessly. The two aircraft carriers were on fire, and he could not land on them. His plane was not equipped with pontoons, and he couldn't come down on the water.

Before his eyes had taken place the greatest disaster in American naval history, and he had been utterly powerless to avert it!

Tim Donovan turned a dread-filled face toward him, asked tremblingly through the earphones: "Jimmy! What—what's it all about?"

Jimmy Christopher gazed down at the fleeing remnants of the United States fleet, and his eyes narrowed. He circled the *Dakota*, then flew to windward of her, and peered through the telescope at the cluster of figures on the bridge. He made out the uniform of Admiral Winston, and beside him that of Captain Loring, the commander of the ship. Just behind them was Lieutenant Ward.

Ward's name had been on that list in Dmitri Osman's possession. Jimmy had feared that Ward might do some physical harm to Admiral Winston at the critical moment, thus leaving the fleet without a supreme command. That might have slowed up the fleet's movements, but would not have proved disastrous. There were plenty of men on those ships who could direct the mighty armada in a sea battle nearly as well as Winston.

But apparently Ward had not harmed the admiral. Something far more subtle—far more devastating—had been consummated under Jimmy Christopher's very eyes. What it was, he could not guess. However, he had seen its effects.

Now he exclaimed to Tim: "They've got enough ships left to stop the Leopard's fleet even now! Why, in God's name, are they falling back?"

There was very little space separating the rearmost of the United States ships from the foremost of the Leopard's fleet. Now, with startling abruptness, a long gun in the forward turret of the Leopard's leading ship belched flame and sound, and a shell screamed through the air, smashing into the stern of a lagging American destroyer. At that close range it had been impossible to miss.

The destroyer's rudder was shattered, and she wallowed suddenly in the trough of the sea, swinging around slowly with her broadside to the leading Asiatic ship.

Jimmy Christopher, flying above the *Dakota*, exulted. Now was the opportunity of the crippled destroyer. A single broadside would blast the pursuing vessel to Kingdom Come. Yet her big guns were silent. She rocked helplessly, and her captain apparently gave no orders as the Asiatic ship steamed up past her and let go with all of her port guns.

The destroyer was raked from stem to stern by that withering broadside, and abruptly Jimmy Christopher's throat became parched. For he saw the United States ensign being hauled down from the staff of the destroyer. She was surrendering without firing a shot!

Such a thing, to Operator 5's knowledge, had never before occurred in American naval history! His hand shook a little as he fingered the controls and banked, coming around into the wind and returning toward the *Dakota*.

Tim Donovan's face was white under the flying helmet and goggles. He brought his lips close to the transmitter, exclaimed: "God, Jimmy! They're quitting cold! Look! There's the flag coming down on another ship!" The boy closed his eyes to hide the sight.

He opened them again, looked back toward Jimmy Christopher. "What's the matter with Winston? He's watching those ships strike their colors and not even making a move to do anything about it!"

It was true. The admiral was standing on the bridge there

beside Captain Loring. He was watching the surrender of the two ships and not moving. As the autogyro passed directly over the flagship, Jimmy Christopher looked squarely down, saw that the admiral's shoulders seemed to droop with despondency. The plane was quite low, and Jimmy could see the listless glance that Winston threw upward at them.

Suddenly Operator 5's lips narrowed into a thin line. His eyes mirrored quick resolve as he barked into the transmitter: "Take over the controls, Tim!"

The boy looked around very startled. "W-what're you going to do, Jimmy?"

"I'm going to bail out! I've got to talk to Winston, and see what's the trouble with him!"

"But Jimmy—!"

"Take over, Tim! Orders!"

OPERATOR 5'S voice crackled with authority, and Tim Donovan turned reluctantly, tested the controls. The boy had been trained to fly by Jimmy Christopher, and he held a pilot's license by special dispensation of the Department of Commerce, even though he was not of age. And he could fly rings around many seasoned airmen.

"Get me altitude!" Jimmy snapped.

In response to his command, the plane rose under Tim Donovan's manipulation, while Operator 5 tightened the cinches of the parachute about himself.

From one of the Asiatic ships, an anti-aircraft gun began to spit; then another and another. The air about the plane began to be peppered with lead.

Calmly, in spite of the air-barrage, Jimmy Christopher threw a leg over the side of the cockpit, waited while Tim maneuvered the autogyro into position at a spot well ahead of the swiftly retreating *Dakota*. Half a dozen of the Asiatic ships were now joining in the fusillade. A slug sang through a wing of the plane, another screeched along one of the struts, but did not break it.

Tim glanced back at Operator 5, cried frantically into the transmitter: "You can't make it, Jimmy! They'll get you sure on the way down!"

But Jimmy Christopher didn't hear; for he had just then ripped off the earphones, thrown his other leg over the side, and kicked away from the plane. Tim's anxious eyes followed him as he plummeted down, and the boy uttered a short prayer.

His heart stopped in his mouth until he saw Jimmy Christopher pull the rip-cord, saw the bag billow and open, saw Jimmy's drop suddenly broken.

Operator 5 had fallen unscathed through the barrage, and now the antiaircraft guns followed him down. He was an easier target than the plane.

Tim Donovan, looking down, saw the muzzles of the long, thin guns on the Asiatic ship lower, to get Operator 5 in range. He said under his breath: "God, Jimmy, they'll get you!"

He saw the tracers from below scorching closer and closer to the parachute. In a moment now they would have the range. The chute was moving down so slowly that they'd be able to pick off Jimmy Christopher at their leisure.

And Tim Donovan, his face white, shouted defiantly down: "Damn you! You *won't* get him!" With sudden decision, he snapped off the autogyro control, flung the plane downward in a singing power dive at the Asiatic fleet. The two machine guns mounted on the wings of the plane burst out in a wicked stutter as he pressed the trips, and a hail of lead spattered the deck of the foremost of the Leopard's ships. Tim flew low, keeping the machine guns belching until the last moment; then he pulled the plane out of the dive and rose swiftly.

His trick worked. The guns on all of the Asiatic ships swung away from the easy target offered by Operator 5, and concentrated on the autogyro. Tim had drawn their fire in order to give Jimmy Christopher a chance to get down!

Once more Tim dived; once more he swept the decks of the enemy ship with hot lead; and again he climbed steeply at the fag end of the dive. The air around him seemed literally filled with leaden death. Holes appeared in a hundred places in the plane. A strut snapped with a sound that was audible even above the roar of the motors.

But the boy, with his young face set in stubborn lines, returned again to dive. But he held his hand on the controls. For his downward glance at the parachute showed him Jimmy Christopher dropping squarely on the deck of the *Dakota!*

He yelled jubilantly into space: "Made it, Jimmy! Atta-boy!" He saw Jimmy Christopher get up out of the tangled mess of the chute, aided by some of the seamen on the deck. Jimmy looked up, and waved to Tim.

The boy leaned far out over the side of the ship, and shook hands with himself in the air. Then, his face all a-grin, he snapped on the autogyro controls, and the huge blades overhead resumed their rhythmic movement. Tim swung the plane about, lifted it high out of the range of the barrage and climbed slowly.

Down below, on the *Dakota*, Jimmy Christopher hastened up to the bridge. As he passed along the decks he noted the expressions of the seamen and the marines. Their faces were dazed, uncomprehending. Most of them paid no attention to Operator 5. They were looking out to sea, watching boarding parties from the Asiatic ships taking over command of the United States vessels which had struck their colors.

When Jimmy Christopher reached the bridge, he strode wrathfully past several officers, faced Admiral Winston.

"Look here, sir!" he exclaimed. "You are throwing this battle

THE LEOPARD

to the Leopard! Even now, you have more ships left than he
has. Why don't you turn on him? You haven't fired a shot yet!"
ADMIRAL WINSTON stood there dejectedly, a beaten
man. Beside him, Captain Loring seemed no more spirited. The
commander of the *Dakota* did not even appear to hear what
Jimmy had said to the admiral. Instead, he threw a frightened
glance in the direction of the pursuing ships of the Asiatic fleet,
and turned to the engine room telegraph. He pressed a button,
spoke into the tube:

"Can't you get more steam up, Michaels?" he demanded of the engineer. "They're still gaining on us!"

Then he turned back, stared out over the bridge at the dreadful scene behind them on the sea. United States ships were floating in flames behind them. Other ships were being boarded by the enemy. Not an American plane was left in the air. All around, behind them, the waters were dotted with the wreckage of those planes—twisted masses of metal and fabric which had plunged into the water at the command of some invisible force.

The anti-aircraft guns had ceased the snarling, but other guns on the enemy ships had opened up now, and shells were falling all about the *Dakota* and the other fleeing vessels.

Admiral Winston's eyes seemed glazed, expressionless, as he faced Jimmy Christopher. Behind the admiral, Lieutenant Ward gazed out at the scene with a dull, listless face.

Operator 5 stepped close to the admiral, seized his coat in one hand, shook him. "Winston!" he cried. "Don't you hear me? What's the matter with you? Look at those ships firing at us! Turn around, man, and put up a fight! Our guns are superior to theirs. We have a longer range! You can still smash that Asiatic fleet!"

Winston shook his head slowly, hopelessly. "It's no use, Operator 5. It's no use! We can never fight the Leopard. Our only hope is to escape!"

The other officers clustered about the rail, paying no attention to Jimmy's hot words, but staring listlessly out over the ocean, their sole thought seeming to be of escape.

Jimmy Christopher's hand dropped from the admiral's coat.

His eyes reflected puzzlement, bewilderment. These men were all brave men, he knew. They had distinguished themselves in many naval engagements during the war. The very men who stood there—the captain and officers of the *Dakota*—had run a submarine blockade into the Mediterranean half a dozen times, convoying troops to Europe. The *Dakota* had been chosen as the flagship of the Atlantic fleet because its crew had signalized itself by its valor in standing off an enemy squadron in the Mediterranean for sixteen hours only a couple of months ago, while the transports it was convoying made port safely. Yet here they were, turning tail meekly without firing a shot, and fleeing from an enemy which had not fired a single shot at them until just now.

Impulsively, Jimmy Christopher turned to Captain Loring. "You, captain!" he urged. "You're a hero to the American public. If you turn tail now, running away like this without firing a shot, you'll go home in disgrace. Give the order to turn around and fight, Captain. I'm sure the other ships will follow your example!"

Loring's face was white with some unnamed dread. "We can't fight!" he groaned hoarsely. "We don't mind dying; but we can't fight something we don't understand!"

THE HEAVY guns of the Asiatic fleet were thundering behind them. The cruiser, *Star*, next in line to the *Dakota*, was suddenly struck by a shell. The shell hit the rear gun-turret, doing little damage against the heavy armor-plate. Yet almost at once the *Star's* flag began to come down!

Winston turned away from Jimmy Christopher, said in a

dazed voice to Lieutenant Ward: "Do you think we should strike our colors too? It's so hopeless—"

Operator 5's face was set, his eyes bleak. He seized Winston by the shoulder, swung him around roughly.

"You're mad, Winston!" he shouted. "You've got more strength than the Leopard. Look at that fleet of his—there are not more than ten ships of war; the rest are transports. Didn't you say that you could blast them out of the water in no time? Go ahead and do it! Give the signal to the fleet to stand and fight!"

Winston gazed at him with dull eyes. "I was mistaken, Operator 5. No man can stand against the Leopard. The less opposition we give him, the better it will be for us—and for the whole country!"

"Damn you!" Jimmy Christopher cried, "You're yellow!" He pushed past the admiral and Captain Loring, stared down onto the deck at the massed men below. They were all looking up at the bridge with pallid, fear-ridden faces.

Operator 5 called out to them: "Men! Your officers are mad. They are throwing this fight. Are you going to let them? By running away now, you are delivering your wives and daughters to the mercy of the Leopard. Will you fight? Then let's take over the ship—"

He got no farther than that. Behind him he heard Captain Loring order: "Seize him!"

He swung about, but too late. There was a rush of feet, and the dozen officers on the bridge overwhelmed him. He struck out with both fists, desperately, madly. For a moment they gave back before the fierceness of his attack.

He stepped quickly to the rail again, shouted down to the men below:

"Come on up, men! Take the ship! Let's put up a fight!"

But the men below stood about listlessly, not moving. And he swung back to the attacking officers just in time to see Lieutenant Ward aiming at him with a revolver from behind Admiral Winston's back. He ducked, launched himself at Ward. But the revolver in the lieutenant's hand bucked, roared. If Jimmy had been standing still at the moment, the slug from that gun would have struck him between the eyes. As it was, his leap saved his life. The slug tore through his flying helmet, creased the top of his skull. Jimmy fell full length on the deck, lay there still. Blood oozed from the top of his head.

The big guns of the Asiatic fleet continued to boom, as Ward calmly put his revolver away, said coolly to Winston:

"That disposes of him, sir. Now we had better try to get away before they sink us."

Winston nodded eagerly, said to Loring: "Get that engineer of yours to coax more steam out of her, Captain."

Loring saluted, turned to obey. And far above them, Tim Donovan in the autogyro, put down the binocular telescopes with which he had been watching the scene on the deck of the *Dakota*, while tears of chagrin coursed down his youthful cheeks. He shook his little fist down at the sea with impotent rage.

"Jimmy!" he sobbed. "Jimmy! They've killed you, Jimmy. God, they've killed you!" His hands shook on the controls as he raced back for shore....

CHAPTER 7
AMERICA IS DOOMED!

IT WAS toward evening that the crippled remnants of the American fleet steamed into New York harbor past the Statue of Liberty, which seemed to stare at them in sardonic bitterness as they filed by. Some thirty-odd ships were all that was left of the majestic fleet which had sailed out so confidently to meet an inferior enemy that morning....

New Yorkers, drawn and gray of face, lined the Battery and the banks of the Hudson, staring uncomprehendingly at these iron-and-steel bulwarks of their safety, which had proved to be no bulwarks at all.

Tim Donovan had returned hours ago, bringing word of the debacle, and now the boy sat tense and white-lipped in that same room in the Custom House where Jimmy Christopher had brought Katerina Saratoff that morning. He was telling the story of what he had seen to the Secretary of War, to General Falk, and to another man. This other man was the black-eyed, square-jawed head of the United States Intelligence Service, known as Z-7. He was Operator 5's chief.

The three men listened to Tim's tale in unbelieving wonder.

"I tell you—" the boy's voice almost broke—"I saw it with my own eyes. I saw the ships haul down their flags, and I saw Jimmy shot. They were fighting on the bridge, and one of the officers with Admiral Winston pulled out a gun and shot him!"

Z-7 got up and paced nervously up and down the room. "After all this!" he muttered. "To think that Operator 5 would be killed by our own men!" He turned to the Secretary of War and General Falk. "That young man was like a son to me. His father served under me. Now his father's in the hospital—and Jimmy is dead!"

The Secretary of War shrugged. "I sympathize with you, Z-7. But there are graver things for us to consider. It appears that Operator 5 was right when he warned us of the Leopard's power. We laughed at him this morning. Now, if he were alive, he could laugh at us."

Tim Donovan got up, his lower lip trembling. The boy was trying hard to restrain his emotion. "Jimmy wouldn't laugh at you, Mr. Secretary. He would *do* something! Look!" Tim pointed dramatically out the window, from which a view of the Upper Bay was afforded. There, under their eyes, was the spectacle of the fleet, limping into port.

Behind the United States ships appeared a line of strange vessels. "There they come!" Tim exclaimed. "The Leopard's fleet! Why do you sit here? Why don't you do something? Are you going to let them take New York?"

General Falk stirred, got up and came to the window.

"They won't take New York," he said with confidence. "The fleet will make a stand in the harbor. Every fort in the harbor and on Staten Island, as well as the coast defense, is just waiting for my signal to open up. We—"

The general stopped short, and his face went pale. "God!" he exclaimed. He reached to the desk, snatched up a telescope, and raised it to his eye. The others in the room clustered around him.

"The fleet is surrendering!" he said hoarsely. "Look at that!"

The others didn't need the telescope to see the flag coming down on the *Dakota*. In a moment the other ships of the fleet followed suit. There, practically within the harbor of New York, the remnants of the country's sea-forces were striking their colors.

"It's uncanny!" Falk murmured. "I would never have thought it of Winston. I've seen that man fight. He's never been afraid of anything in his life. And now—"

HE SWUNG away from the window. The Secretary of War took the telescope from him with a trembling hand, applied it to his eye. Tim Donovan crowded up beside the portly cabinet officer, and watched the American ships heave to; each with its flag lowered, and await the slow, steady approach of the Asiatic fleet.

The Secretary suddenly thrust the telescope at Tim, rushed to the phone on the table. "I've got to call Washington—"

But he was roughly pushed aside by General Falk, who growled at him:

"Washington can wait! This is more pressing!" And he seized the phone, barked a number into it. When he got his connection he snapped:

"Falk talking! Give the signal for Forts Wood and Jay to open up at once on the enemy fleet in the harbor. Have them flood the bay with shells! Bring every gun to bear on those ships. And they needn't worry about our own vessels. Understand? And they're not to stop until I give the word. I'll be watching!"

He put down the phone, turned to the others with a saturnine smile. "Watch the fireworks now!" he said. "The gunners at those forts have been waiting for the signal for an hour. In one minute the bombardment will begin. The Leopard and his fleet have sailed into a trap!"

He pushed past the Secretary of War, and stepped to the window beside Tim Donovan. The Secretary peered over his shoulder, while Z-7 went to the next window.

Everybody in the room was at high tension. The thoughts of Z-7 and of Tim Donovan were divided between the peril that threatened the city, and the fate which had overtaken Operator 5. They all watched, dull-eyed, the dramatic scene in the Bay, almost within the shadow of the Statue of Liberty, and of Fort Wood, on Bedloe Island. Boarding parties had left several of the vessels in the Asiatic Fleet, and were moving toward the American ships, which were awaiting them docilely.

Falk chuckled, deep in his throat. "Thirty seconds more," he said, "and you will see what I mean by a trap. These ships are right under the guns of Fort Wood on Bedloe Island, and of Fort Jay on Governor's Island. They won't be there five minutes after the bombardment opens. Mr. Leopard doesn't seem to know that it is impossible to attack New York Harbor. I've spent ten years making it impregnable. Our coast defense guns, together with the batteries in the forts can sink anything that floats before it gets to the Battery!"

He reached for the telescope which Tim was using, saying gruffly: "Here, boy. I'll take—"

Tim interrupted him with a hoarse shout, jerked the glass out of the general's grasp, and kept his eye at it. "Jimmy!" he shouted. "It's Jimmy! He's just dived off the *Dakota!*" The lad turned around, his eyes shining with sudden relief and joy, and he almost screamed at Z-7: "It's Jimmy, I tell you! I saw his face as he jumped!"

The others, also, had seen the lone figure race down the ladder from the bridge to the deck of the *Dakota,* leap over the side. They had not recognized the man, of course, but Tim had been focusing his glass on the flagship, in an effort to find the body of Operator 5. Now he almost danced with joy.

Falk scowled, attempted to take the telescope from him, but the boy pushed the general aside, peered through it again. He followed the swimming figure as it stroked powerfully away from the *Dakota,* while Z-7 breathed a deep sigh of relief. The news that Jimmy Christopher was still alive had removed a heavy load from his heart.

But General Falk growled: "Too bad. Ten seconds to go. When the bombardment starts, Operator 5 won't have a chance. Even if he isn't directly hit, the detonation will stun him. He'll sink!"

Tim Donovan turned quickly, gripped the general's sleeve. His eyes were desperate, and his lips were trembling. "Please, General!" he begged. "Hold off on the bombardment for a couple of minutes. He's a strong swimmer. Give him a fighting chance to get away. Quick! You still have time to phone!"

FALK SHOOK his head. "Sorry, boy. I know how you feel. But we can't let one man's life stand in our way now. Operator 5 will have to take his medicine. I'd sacrifice a thousand lives—I'm doing it anyway—in order to blast that Asiatic Fleet out of the harbor. I'm sacrificing the lives of every man in our own ships. I can't—"

Tim Donovan sobbed hysterically, beat with his fists against Falk's uniformed breast. "Damn you! Damn you!" he shouted. "You never liked Jimmy. Now you're willing to see him die. Well, you won't!"

Out in the harbor the lone swimmer cut through the water lithely, swiftly. In the room, Falk staggered backward under the boy's sudden onslaught, his face purple with rage.

Abruptly Tim sprang away from him, scooped up the phone from the desk. "Give me Corps Headquarters!" he snapped into the instrument.

Falk demanded: "What are you going to do?" and leaped toward him.

Tim Donovan's eyes were blazing. He reached into the open drawer of the desk, where he saw a service revolver lying, and snatched it out, leveled it at General Falk. "Stand back!" he shouted. "I'll kill you if you try to stop me!"

Falk stopped stock-still at the wild look in Tim's eyes. He knew that the boy would shoot.

Into the telephone Tim spoke rapidly: "Corps Headquarters! General Falk wishes to countermand the order to open bombardment. You will delay it ten minutes, then open—"

He stopped speaking as Z-7 came around the desk, behind him, and struck down the wrist in which he held the revolver. Falk jumped in and snatched it away, clubbed it to bring it down on Tim's head. But Z-7 blocked the blow.

Falk glared at the Intelligence Chief. "Look out of my way! I'll break that whelp's neck—"

"You'll do nothing!" Z-7 snapped at him. "Don't you see

that the lad is crazy with fear?" He glanced down at Tim, who had collapsed on the desk, sobbing with deep rasping sobs that racked his young body. He put his hand on the boy's shoulder.

"Timmy!" he said softly. "It had to be this way. Jimmy would have wanted it like this if he'd been asked. I'd gladly die in his place if I could—"

Falk had grasped the telephone, and was barking into it:

"Proceed as I ordered, Lieutenant Gormley. Let the bombardment commence without delay. Have you given the order... *what?*"

Tim Donovan stopped his sobbing, raised his head at the sudden urgency—the sudden hint of panic—in the general's voice.

The Secretary of War stepped closer, demanded sharply: "What's the matter, Falk?"

But the Chief of Staff didn't answer. He listened to a staccato voice at the other end, then shouted into the transmitter: "Put me through directly to Colonel Sloane at Fort Wood. Why! the—the—" Falk seemed to choke on the sudden anger that filled him. He stuttered for a moment, swallowed hard, then roared into the phone: "I'll hold the line! Put me right through!"

While he waited for the connection he sputtered with rage.

Z-7 glanced at Tim Donovan, said quietly: "I don't think you need to worry about Jimmy."

The Secretary of War demanded again: "What is the meaning of all this, Falk? You said the bombardment would commence in one minute. It's more than two minutes now—"

Falk tried to keep calm. His hand squeezed so hard on the

80

telephone that it seemed the instrument would be snapped in two. He said tightly: "Colonel Sloane, at Fort Wood, informs Lieutenant Gormley that he thinks it's no use to bombard the Leopard's fleet. He says it's hopeless to try to defend New York against the invasion. *He won't fight!*"

The Secretary took a step backward as if he had been struck a blow. He echoed Falk's words. "Won't fight? But—but—!"

He stopped as Falk got his connection, fairly roared into the phone:

"Sloane! What's happened to you over there? Are you mad? Get your guns in action, I tell you. Hurry man! You…*oh my God!*" Falk's voice broke. Tim and Z-7, who were quite close to the general, distinctly heard the click at the other end, as Colonel Sloane hung up on his superior.

All the energy seemed to go out of Falk. He sighed, and let the phone drop from listless hands. "We're licked!" he said in a very low voice. "Sloane is quitting on the job. Gormley tells me that the commanders of Wadsworth and Hamilton won't fight either. The coast defense are lying down, too. They all say the same thing—that it's no use trying to fight the Leopard!"

TIM STARED at him with wet, red eyes. "Jimmy Christopher warned you that something like this would happen. Didn't he tell you that the Leopard had marched across Russia without opposition? Didn't he tell you the same thing would happen here? But you wouldn't listen to him! Maybe you'll listen to him now!"

The boy sprang to the window. Night had fallen swiftly. It was too dark to be able to make out anything on the waters of the bay. If Operator 5 were still swimming, it was impossible to catch sight of him.

There were red lights on the ships, now, and Tim shuddered as he saw the ominous Leopard flag go up on one after another of the American vessels as the boarding parties reached them.

The Secretary of War watched over Tim's shoulder. "There's no more United States Navy!" he whispered. He swung on Falk. "Those ships of the Leopard will land their troops in the morning. We've got to organize a defense. We've got to keep them out of New York!"

Falk laughed. "How are we going to keep them out? Our officers won't fight!" His eyes swung to Z-7, who had picked up the telephone and was talking quietly into it. When the Intelligence chief hung up, Falk asked him sarcastically: "Well, what are you doing to save your country from invasion? Or do you think we ought to retreat before the Leopard the way the Russians did?"

Z-7 replied without rancor. "We seem to be at a standstill. You appear helpless. I've phoned some of my men to get out in the harbor and try to pick up Operator 5. I confess I don't know what steps to suggest next. Perhaps he will know what to do."

Falk grimaced. "I'll not wait for that. I'm going to order all the troops available into New York. The Leopard can't land till morning. By then we'll have a reception ready for him!"

Z-7 laughed bitterly. "The only trained troops in the area embarked this morning—against the advice of Operator 5, I understand. They're out at sea now, waiting for a convoy which will never arrive. Where are you going to get troops?"

"I'll get them… somewhere!" Falk said stubbornly. "We're not reduced yet to waiting for the advice of a young whippersnapper like your Operator 5!"

The Secretary of War frowned. He leaned his stout, soft body against the window sill, stared out moodily at the ships clustered in the bay. "I can't understand this," he said querulously. "What could Winston have learned that caused him to turn tail and retreat? And what can have happened to Sloane and the commanders of the other forts in the bay, to make them feel it's useless to fight? I've got to call the President, and God help me. I don't know what to tell him!"

"Tell him," Z-7 said harshly, "that he will soon be a president without a country. Tell him that within forty-eight hours he will see the United States laid waste the way Russia was; that he will see his country pillaged and raped and burned—if he leaves its defense in the present hands!" Z-7's chin jutted. "And if you don't tell him that, I will, by God!"

General Falk's face flushed a deep red, and his hands clenched. He took a single step forward, and stopped, facing the Intelligence Chief. The two men stood that way for a long minute, their eyes locked, wills clashing.

In a moment there might have been a physical clash between the two. But just then the telephone rang. Without taking his eyes from Z-7, Falk picked it up and answered it. Then he handed it sullenly to Z-7. The Intelligence Chief took the instrument, said: "Yes?" and listened for a second. His eyes brightened. "See that he has dry clothes," he ordered, "and bring him right up here!"

He put down the phone, exclaimed excitedly: "They've picked up Operator 5! He's safe! Now—"

His words were drowned by the dull boom of cannonading. Flashes of fire shone from Governor's Island, out in the harbor. They all rushed to the window. Thunderous detonations reverberated through the air, deafening them. Huge projectiles screamed high over their heads, above the roof of the Custom House Building. The night was suddenly made garish with flame and fire and noise.

The three men and the boy looked out at the harbor, standing in speechless amazement; terror rushed upon them as they realized what was happening.

Z-7 exclaimed in choked horror: "The Leopard has taken Fort Jay! They've turned our guns against us. They're bombarding the city!"

CHAPTER 8
THE LEOPARD'S FIRST BLOW

WITHIN TWENTY minutes after the bombardment began, New York City became untenable. The enemy had not stopped at the capture of Fort Jay. They had taken, in swift sequence, Forts Wood, Hamilton and Wadsworth. The big guns of these forts, together with the heavy pieces of the surrendered ships, belched a continuous torrent of steel into the metropolis.

The Leopard seemed to be bent upon making a shambles of Manhattan Island, and he succeeded. Shells fell everywhere, spreading destruction and devastation. Almost at once the great exodus began. Every means of conveyance was used to hurry frantic, terror-stricken civilians to safety. But those who perished far outnumbered those who escaped.

All the main arteries leading out of Manhattan were clogged with autos of all vintages and descriptions. Household goods were abandoned. Trucks labored under loads of fifty and sixty people apiece. Private cars were crowded to capacity. The few regular soldiers available in the city, as well as the National Guard, were hastily impressed to aid the police in keeping traffic moving northward into Westchester, and across the Hudson into Jersey.

General Falk had acted with speed and efficiency. In spite of his choleric temper and hide-bound, old-school methods, he was a brave man, capable of quick decisions. He had only a few minutes after the commencement of the rain of steel projectiles in which to issue orders. After that, the telephones and the lighting systems were paralyzed.

It was characteristic of him that he was big enough to acknowledge his mistakes when he was finally convinced of them; and when Jimmy Christopher burst into the room in the Custom House, dripping wet, not having waited to change clothes, the general was the first to meet him at the door.

"Operator 5," he said steadily, "I've been an old fool. Everything you predicted has come to pass." Falk's face was suddenly lined and old. "If we shouldn't survive this night, I want to say here and now that I am the one to blame!"

He had to shout to make himself heard above the thunder

The steady shelling lasted five hours and left Manhattan a graveyard....

of the guns and the crashing explosions in the city where the big shells fell.

Jimmy Christopher passed a wet hand across his face, and wrung water from his flying suit. He was panting, breathing hard from his long swim. There was a raw welt across the top of his head, where Ward's bullet had creased him. He was weary, almost dropping from his wound and from exhaustion. But his eyes still flashed with the energy that kept him going even while his body screamed to him from every muscle for rest.

He brushed Falk's self-criticism aside. "You're not to blame, General. You couldn't be expected to believe that anything like this could happen. Now we've got to face it. You must use every available man in uniform. All cars and trucks must be commandeered, and the city of New York must be evacuated. God knows if we'll be able to get a tenth of the people out of here alive!"

Falk nodded eagerly, rushed to the telephone. He issued swift orders, then listened while Jimmy swiftly outlined more things that had to be done.

"We must keep communications open. In a little while, the telephone lines will be down, and the light cables will be destroyed. A shell may strike a vital spot at any time. Arrange for communication by flares and very lights. Get in touch with Forts Slocum and Schuyler in Westchester, with Fort Tilden in Rockaway, and Totten in Bayside. They all have the range of the harbor. Have them open up at once."

Falk nodded, talked swiftly into the phone. He got the machinery of transportation in motion, then called Fort Tilden. Just as he got the connection, the line went dead. He dropped the phone, made a gesture of resignation. "That's that. I'll have to send messengers now." He turned to the Secretary of War. "You'd better be getting out, sir. This building may be hit any minute. All of you—"he waved a hand to include Tim Donovan and Z-7—"come out of here."

HE LED the way down to the street. Outside, though night had set in, there was plenty of light to see by. Fires had started in a hundred places throughout the city, and the flames made the darkness bright. The din of the cannonading deafened them, and the screeching of the shells made a continuous unearthly sound that dinned into their brains.

Men and women were running about wildly, panic-stricken. They had come down here to the Battery to see the fleet come back victorious. Instead, they had witnessed its abject surrender. Even when they saw the gruesome flag of the Leopard on the pursuing ships—even when they saw that flag go up on the captured United States vessels—they had not fully realized their own peril. Now, with the city in flames, with the continuous booming of cannon, their minds refused to react to the full significance of the catastrophe. They milled about on the Battery and in Bowling Green, like so many sheep, waiting for a shell to descend upon them and wipe them out of existence.

In response to Falk's orders, automobiles began to pour into the square, driven by National Guardsmen, and the terror-stricken people were loaded into them, packed like sardines, and driven quickly across to the East River, where ferries carried them over to Queens and the remoter parts of Brooklyn.

All the bridges were jammed. One of the first shells struck

the Williamsburg Bridge, and the mighty structure buckled, collapsed into the river carrying with it thousands of unfortunates who had been seeking safety. After that, no one would use the remaining bridges to Queens and Brooklyn, and as a result, the ferries were overloaded. One ferry foundered in crossing, and hundreds more perished.

Soon the streets became impassable with debris from collapsed buildings. Huge craters appeared in the asphalt where shells struck. Water mains burst, flooding the whole of Manhattan Island. Gas fumes filled the air, mingling with the smell of cordite.

At Times Square, where there was an intricate network of subway lines underground, the whole surface caved in from the west side of Seventh Avenue to the east side of Broadway, and from Forty-second to Forty-fourth street. The Times Building and the Paramount Theatre Building collapsed, as well as many smaller structures in the area. The exact loss of life was never ascertained.

At last it became impossible for vehicles to move out of the city, due to the broken-up streets. Those who had not escaped with the first wave of the exodus, and who were unable to find accommodations on any of the ferries, were doomed to remain and die. And die they did.

After five hours of steady shelling, the bombardment suddenly ceased. There was now no sign of life anywhere in the streets. Of the almost two million souls who had inhabited the borough of Manhattan, it was estimated that less than two hundred thousand had escaped the holocaust. The scorched, twisted, charred, drowned bodies of the other million eight hundred thousand persons made of Manhattan Island the greatest graveyard in the world.

At a single stroke, as many people had been wiped out as the United States had sent overseas to the trenches of Europe. And now the pitifully depleted troops gathered in Westchester, in Long Island and in Jersey, prepared to make a stand against the invaders.

The Secretary of War had flown to Washington in Jimmy Christopher's autogyro, with a pilot whom General Falk had supplied.

Jimmy himself, with the general, Tim Donovan and Z-7, remained in Manhattan until the last moment; all three of them kept constantly on the move, exerting themselves tirelessly to save the last possible human being from the terrific barrage that was being laid down. The section around the Battery had not been as heavily hit as other parts, and they were able to stall almost until the end of the bombardment. It was from an improvised headquarters that General Falk issued orders by means of runner and signal, for the concentration of what troops there were at hand around the Kensico Dam in Westchester, around Forest Park in Queens, and along the Palisades on the Jersey shore.

IT WAS at Jimmy Christopher's recommendation that he chose those sites, each of them being ideal for defense by a small body of men.

At last, bursting water mains flooded them out of Bowling

91

Green, and they moved eastward just as the first of the Leopard's ships moved up the Hudson with the dawn.

Forts Schuyler, Slocum and Totten, as well as Tilden in Rockaway, had laid down a barrage in the harbor, but had done little damage to the enemy ships, for they had moved about constantly, without lights. Observation planes sent up from every field had been able to render little help in range-finding, due to the darkness. A couple of hits had been scored on Bedloe Island, but not at the fort; the right arm of the Statue of Liberty had been struck, falling in a shattered mass of metal. One or two of the enemy ships had been struck by accident, but aside from that, the Leopard's fleet was unscathed through the night.

With the coming of dawn, a flock of airplanes went up at Falk's command, but no sooner had they appeared over the Asiatic Fleet, than they began to act as erratically as had those attached to Winston's squadrons. Some mysterious power wielded by the Leopard seemed to deprive the pilots of their faculties, and the planes crashed into each other in the air, took nose dives, and went into tailspins until they struck the water.

After the destruction of the first contingent, Falk ordered no more air observation. It was at this time that he decided to leave Manhattan and take over command of the forces he had concentrated in Westchester.

"We'll make our stand around the Kensico Dam," he told Jimmy. "If this damn voodoo of the Leopard's should, by any chance, work up there, we'll be able to smash the dam and flood him out. It'll mean a terrific waste of land, and it'll do irreparable damage; but it'll all be nothing to what's already been done!"

Jimmy Christopher had worked like a beaver with the general, as had Tim and Z-7. But through it all there had preyed on Jimmy's mind the thought of his father in Mercy Hospital, and of Diane and Katerina with him. The hospital must have been destroyed with everything else. There was a queer heaviness in his chest when he stopped for a moment to think of that, but he said nothing, knowing that the same thing must be in the minds of Z-7 and Tim Donovan.

At last, the general was ready to leave by the power boat which awaited him at the foot of Liberty Street, on the East River. He said to Operator 5: "All right, I guess there's nothing more we can do here. We can't help the dead. The power boat will take us up the river around Astoria to the Glenn Curtiss Airport. I've got a plane waiting there to fly us to the Kensico Dam. Let's go—"

"Just a minute, general," Jimmy Christopher said quietly. "You go with Tim and Z-7. I'm staying here."

Falk stared at him. "Staying here! Why, man, the Leopard's troops will land here in an hour. You'll be taken—"

"I've got to stay, General," Jimmy persisted. "You know in your heart that all these plans you're making aren't worth a tinker's damn. The Leopard has some kind of power that makes our men quit before they start. How do you know you'll be immune to it, any more than Winston was, or the commanders of the forts in the bay? Our only chance is to find out what that power is. I'm going to stay and make a try at finding out!"

They were in the street in front of the Custom House Building, and Z-7 stepped up beside Jimmy, said quickly: "I'm stay-ing too!"

Tim Donovan exclaimed: "Atta-boy! The three of us will stay. We can't leave Jimmy here alone. We'll show that Leopard—we'll clip his claws yet!"

GENERAL FALK'S face was gray in the half light of the new morning. His eyes mirrored a strange wistfulness. "You are brave—I almost said 'men'—" with a glance at Tim's slim youthfulness—"The Three Musketeers! I—I wish I could stay here with you. You're right, Operator 5. There's little chance of our making a stand against the Leopard as long as he controls this power to make us quit. There's no use in my taking over command at Kensico; anybody else can surrender just as well as I can." Suddenly a fierce resolve showed in his face. "I'm going to remain here with you! Let me die with you, rather than see our country ravished by this coolie from Asia!"

"No, no!" Jimmy Christopher burst out. "You're needed else-where, sir!" General Falk was an executive whom it would be hard, if not impossible to replace at this time. Though Operator 5 had clashed with him often, he recognized the old war-dog's outstanding ability and innate tenacity. For him to stay here engaged in espionage work, would constitute a fatal loss to the defenses of the country.

"You've got to go, sir!" he rushed on. "This isn't your work; it's ours. Take Tim along with you—he doesn't belong here either. Hurry, sir. Z-7 and I will need time to get under cover and perfect our plans. Come on!" He started to lead the way across the water-swept street, littered with sewage from broken pipes.

But Falk stood his ground stubbornly. "I'm staying with you! Operator 5, I am the Chief of Staff of the United States Army. As such I am the superior of yourself and Z-7. I order you to cease arguing. I'm staying!"

Jimmy turned slowly, throwing a side glance at Z-7. He said: "I admire you for your courage, sir. If I were in your place, I'd want to do the same. But you're needed at Kensico. So, I hope that later on you'll forgive me for this!"

As he spoke he stepped in close, brought up his bunched fist in a swift blow to the point of Falk's jaw. There was a dull thud, and the general sagged, his eyes glazing.

Jimmy caught him before he fell to the ground. "Help me carry him to the boat, Z-7!" he rapped.

The Intelligence Chief was startled at Jimmy's swift action; then suddenly he smiled, bent to help. The two men carried General Falk across the three blocks to the foot of Liberty Street, deposited him in the power boat which was waiting, manned by three officers of the General Staff.

They fired questions at Z-7 and Jimmy Christopher when they saw their chief being carried, unconscious.

"The general's had an accident," Jimmy explained. "He'll be all right in a little while. Take him up to the airport as fast as you can."

The officer in charge, who knew both Z-7 and Operator 5, nodded, and made Falk as comfortable as possible in the stern of the boat.

"Just a minute," Jimmy said. He swung around to Tim Donovan. "All right, kid. Get in there too."

Tim Donovan shook his head rebelliously. "Nix, Jimmy. I go where you go. Laugh that off!"

Jimmy stepped close to Tim, drawing his right arm back a bit, setting himself for another blow. But the boy had learned his lesson from watching what had happened to Falk. He backed away hurriedly, turned and ran down the street. Then, when he got a safe distance away he stopped, and thumbed his nose at Jimmy.

"Come back here!" Jimmy shouted. "Get in that boat or I'll break your neck!"

"Okay, Jimmy!" the lad called back. "Send the boat away, and I'll bring my neck over to be broken!"

JIMMY SHRUGGED helplessly. He nodded to the officer, and the painter was thrown off, the boat chugged up the river bearing the unconscious Chief of Staff.

Z-7 said to Jimmy: "The lad's been through so much with you, he's entitled to stay, Jimmy. I can tell how he feels—with your father and Diane probably dead, with you going into the face of almost certain death; I guess there's nothing left in life for him."

Jimmy nodded somberly. He motioned to Tim, who came running back, but stayed at a respectful distance.

"Fingers, Jimmy?" he asked, watching warily lest Jimmy Christopher make a dive for him.

"Fingers, Tim. I guess you stay."

The boy's face lighted up joyfully, and he came closer. "What do we do now?"

Jimmy glanced questioningly at Z-7. "First of all, we've got to find a place to hole up in till after the Leopard and his men have landed. Has Intelligence got any spots around here that haven't been destroyed?"

Z-7 shook his head. "You know all the Intelligence addresses as well as I do, Jimmy. There's nothing—"

Suddenly Operator 5 snapped his fingers. "I've got just the place! Do you remember the old municipal wine cellars under the Brooklyn Bridge? They haven't been used for years. Hardly anybody knows about them. We could hide out in them for years, and nobody would find us!"

"Wine cellars?" Tim asked. "I never heard of them."

"You've got a lot to learn yet, kid," Jimmy told him.

Z-7's eyes were sparkling. "It's a natural, Jimmy. Maybe we can recruit a force of men down there. There must be some survivors wandering about the city, unable to escape. We can move them in there!"

The three hurried up Broadway, picking their way in the unsure footing of torn-up asphalt and mangled bodies, debris of buildings and floating sewage.

Behind them, the first of the Leopard's ships tied up at the Battery, and a stream of men began to descend. Jimmy Christopher and his two companions glanced back frequently, watching the queerly mailed soldiers from Asia set foot on New York ground. In their van was a huge figure, with a peculiar breastplate of mail, and a helmet of similar material. In the light of the flares which illuminated the landing they could see this huge figure strut up and down while his men disembarked. He carried only a single weapon—a huge Chinese broadsword, which the average man would have required two hands to wield, but which he carried easily in his right fist.

Z-7 whispered to Jimmy: "The Leopard!"

Jimmy Christopher nodded. He half turned, as if to go back. "If we could get him now, the whole invasion would fall to pieces!"

But Z-7 laid a restraining hand on his arm. "Too late, Jimmy. You could never reach him!"

It was true. The immense figure of the Leopard was now completely surrounded by a bodyguard of mailed warriors. Other Asiatic soldiers now descended, wheeling motorcycles. They formed in a solid phalanx ahead of the bodyguard. And so the procession of the conquering horde from Asia marched into the wrecked streets of New York City, while Operator 5, Z-7 and Tim Donovan slunk away before them toward the old wine cellars.

CHAPTER 9
MINUTE MEN OF 1936!

THOUGH MANHATTAN had been turned into a gory shambles, there were yet many spots between the Battery and Spuyten Duyvil which had been spared by the screaming barrage. Here and there, houses stood, untouched. By a peculiar quirk of fate, the old Sixth Avenue Elevated line between South Ferry and Fifty-Third Street had not been hit in its entire length. The old, rickety-looking structure, which the taxpayers of the city had been fighting to tear down for years, still stood intact. Along its entire length the trains of wooden cars remained on the tracks, at the spots where they had stopped when the power-houses ceased to function.

And it was to the shelter of these cars that hundreds of survivors flocked. Men and women without homes, carrying children in their arms, or lugging some few possessions that they had managed to salvage, climbed the creaking staircases of the "L" structure, walked the tracks until they found a car in which there was room for them.

The biting January winds had caught many without clothes, just as they had run from their homes. Some had only thin night clothes to protect them against the bitter winds; and there was none who had clothing to spare. So they hurried gladly to the comparative warmth of the elevated cars.

The stations along the line had been improvised into emergency dressing rooms for the wounded, and here the handful of doctors who had survived were treating victims of the bombardment as well as many patients who had been carried from neighboring hospitals.

As well as they could, without leadership, physicians and nurses had organized a home-made system of relief, scouting among the wreckage of drug stores for medical supplies, gauze and bandages, and using whatever came to hand.

During the early morning hours these unselfish doctors and nurses labored over the sick and wounded, not knowing what their fate was to be, wondering vaguely in the backs of their minds whether the conquerors would not come in a little while and undo with the sword what they had done so well with the implements of the healing arts.

They were soon to know....

At eleven o'clock the first cohorts of the Asiatic army began their march through Manhattan Island. In their van, strangely, rode the Leopard himself, in the armored sidecar of a motorcycle. The streets were impassable to wide-bodied automobiles, but these narrow vehicles, which the Asiatic army had used in Russia, were able to negotiate them with comparative ease, skirting the wide maws of the shell-holes in the asphalt, sloshing through deep puddles of sewage. The stench in the city was almost unbearable, but the Leopard did not seem to mind.

His darting eyes, set deep in his flat head, seemed to look everywhere at once, as if he were savoring to the full the perfume of his victory. In spite of the cold, he wore the same breech-clout that he had worn on the plains of Russia, with the addition of a glinting metal breastplate, and helmet of the same material. His arms, thighs and legs were bare, copper-colored, oily. Muscles bulged on his sinewy body.

Behind him, far down Broadway, was strung out the long line of motorcycles, and behind the motorcycles came infantry, disembarking from ship after ship that tied up at the dock.

Lean, wiry, yellow men these, who marched phlegmatically, stoically, hardly impressed with the sight of the havoc their guns had wrought. Each motorcycle was armed with a machine-gun cunningly fastened to the front plate of the side car, so that it could be swiveled in any direction. The cycles themselves were heavy machines, with solid tires. The driver was protected by a sort of shield which was part of the handle-bar, and which came down in front almost to his knees. It was equipped with slotted holes for the eyes. The only parts of the driver which were exposed were his feet.

As the motorcade proceeded up lower Broadway, patrols branched out from the main column into the side streets wherever they were passable, and then filtered up the other north-and-south thoroughfares. Wherever there appeared to be signs of life, the patrols stopped and investigated....

WHATEVER UNFORTUNATES were found huddled in chance buildings which had been left standing were immediately seized and searched. Then, after any valuables in their possession had been taken from them, they were forced to march north at the double-quick, ahead of the motorcycles. No words were spoken to them by the little yellow soldiers, but resistance or objections of any kind insured swift death.

On the East Side, a patrol found two dozen or so bedraggled men and women, with two children among them, huddled for shelter in one of the loading platforms used by the vegetable markets.

The mailed Asiatics descended from the armored cars, swarmed into the loading platform, and prodded the shivering, frightened captives out into the raw cold night at the points of their bayonets.

Several of the women were only half dressed, and the gallant men had lent them overcoats and other articles of clothing. The overcoats were ruthlessly stripped from the women, and the rough hands of the wiry yellow soldiers searched them for valuables.

One of the women, a plump young matron, pretty, with blond hair, wore only a night dress under the great overcoat which she pressed about her. She shrank from the brutal soldier who ripped the coat open, and turned to cling to a tall man who was holding a curly-headed girl of five by the hand. The little girl was staring with wide, frightened eyes at the silent soldiers. The tall man put his free arm about the woman, shouted at the mailed looters: "Damn you! Take your hands off my wife!"

The soldier grinned wickedly under his helmet, swung his long rifle down, and without hesitation thrust the bright, glinting bayonet into the tall man's stomach, twisted it cruelly, and yanked it out, dripping red.

The tall man screamed, writhing in agony as blood gushed from him, then he collapsed to the ground, his screams dying to muted groans. The little girl whose hand he had been holding stood rooted to the spot, staring with unbelieving eyes at the death throes of her father, while the woman swiftly knelt, grasped at her husband with frantic hands.

She cradled his head in her arms, let her tears fall on his face. The wounded man's hands were pressed hard to his stomach, and they were becoming swiftly wet with his own blood.

The soldiers of the Asiatic patrol were facing the rest of the group of fugitives, holding their bayonets ready for any further protests. But the others were too cowed by what had happened to do anything but stand meekly by. There were six mailed men in that patrol, under the command of a petty officer. It was the officer who had stabbed the woman's husband.

Now he bent down, seized her by the shoulder, and dragged her roughly away from her husband. The man's head fell to the ground as she was suddenly compelled to release him, while the little girl, with a sudden cry of anguish, rushed at the officer, beating at him with her two little fists, and shouting:

"My daddy! You hurt my daddy!"

The Asiatic officer bared his teeth at the child, held the woman with one hand, and raised his clubbed rifle with the other. In another instant he would have brought it down on her skull.

It was at that instant that the bark of an automatic sounded at a little distance behind him. A slug whined through the air, smashed into the bone of his right wrist, shattered it. The rifle fell from inert fingers, and he let go of the screaming woman, gazed stupidly at his bloody hand, which suddenly hung uselessly at his side.

The five men of his detail swung, startled, in the direction from which the shot had come. About fifty feet down the street was a low pile of debris from a shell-torn building, consisting of bricks and fragments of steel which had fallen athwart the gutter. Behind this pile of wreckage they saw the head and shoulders of a young man, attired in a flying suit and helmet. The top of his leather helmet was stained with clotted blood.

Beside the young man stood a grizzled, older man, and on his left hand was a boy with a freckled face. All three of them held automatics.

EVEN AS the yellow soldiers raised their rifles, the young man and his two companions fired again, their automatics spitting flame at the armored warriors. Lead slugs clanged harmlessly against the armor of the Asiatics; their breastplates were bullet-proof. The fusillade did no damage beyond staggering the Asiatics backward, spoiling their aim with the rifles.

Their first volley went high over the heads of the three behind the breastwork of debris. The twenty-odd American captives stood tense with sudden hope as the young man and his two companions fired again, more carefully from behind their protection.

One of the Asiatic soldiers uttered a scream that ended in a gurgling whisper, pitched forward with a jagged hole spurting blood from his throat. Another collapsed on a wounded leg, while a third was spun about by the force of a bullet through the exposed part of his shoulder.

The three with the automatics had realized at once that the armor was not for show, but was truly bullet-proof; and they were aiming at the exposed parts of the Asiatics.

The wounded officer shouted to the two unwounded soldiers in a high-pitched, sing-song dialect, and the two dropped to their knees, took deliberate aim with their rifles. But the young man behind the debris fired twice, quickly, with deadly accuracy, and caught them both between the eyes before they could shoot.

A glad shout went up from the shivering white captives, and the Asiatic officer, suddenly gripped with fear, turned to run, holding his shattered wrist pressed close to his chest. But the little girl, who had been standing at the side of her dying father, threw herself at him, clasping his shins in both her frail arms. The officer went sprawling to the ground, and in a moment the three had run out from behind the breastworks and leaped upon him.

In a few minutes, the four wounded Asiatics were securely tied with belts and suspenders commandeered from the men among the fugitives. The young man with the automatic patted the little girl on the head.

"That was a brave thing you did, young lady," he said.

She looked up at him, smiling through her tears, then glanced at the trembling form of her mother, leaning over the rigid body of her father.

"Daddy!" she called in choked voice. "Daddy!"

Gently the young man led her away from the sight. He called over the freckle-faced boy, who had been busy examining the armor and weapons of the fallen Asiatics.

"Here's something for you to do, Tim," he said. "Take care of this young lady. She needs care."

Tim Donovan grimaced, but took over the assignment without other objection.

Z-7 was talking to the bedraggled fugitives, and Jimmy Christopher went over to him, said crisply: "I have an idea, Chief. Let's get all these people into the shelter of the wine cellar. Have them help to carry the Asiatics in there too. We can use that armor and those rifles."

He turned to the assembled group. "It's a lucky thing this happened right around the corner from our hiding place. We heard the motorcycles, and came out to investigate. Now, if you'll help us carry these prisoners around the corner, we'll get them in there and mop up around here, so as not to leave any trace of what's happened in case another patrol should come along. Then I've got a little plan to talk over with all of you. I suppose you'd all be willing to strike a blow against the Leopard?"

The men in the group assured him fervently that they would. The wife of the man who had been bayoneted came over, pressing the overcoat about her, her eyes shining with a fanatic glow.

"I'll help," she said. "They killed my husband."

The statement was a simple one, and she said it without any great show of emotion. But Jimmy Christopher could detect the taut hate behind her eyes.

"You shall have your chance, madam," he promised. "Meanwhile, you can help best by taking care of your little girl." He motioned to Tim Donovan, who led the child over, gave her into the custody of her mother.

IT WAS the work of only a short while for the men and women of that group to carry the wounded Asiatic soldiers around the corner, and to dispose of the body of the dead father and the two yellow soldiers whom Jimmy had shot between the eyes. Soon there was nothing to show that anything had happened at this spot except for several dull, reddish stains in the gutter.

Around the corner was the entrance to the old wine cellars. Above them loomed the wrecked structure of the Brooklyn Bridge, with long shanks of steel hanging from the splintered framework. All about them were the torn and twisted bodies of civilians who had died during the bombardment, half covered by debris from the destroyed bridge.

Through all this wreckage Jimmy Christopher led the way to a shattered subway kiosk. Picking his way through twisted steel, he found the staircase leading down into the subway station. Behind him came a procession of bedraggled men and women, carrying the wounded Asiatics. Into the eyes of these people had come a new light of hope. Jimmy's quiet, efficient manner, his crisp, quick decisiveness, had imbued them with fresh courage.

At the end of the procession, Z-7 and Tim Donovan, with one of the men from the fugitive group, wheeled the three motorcycles. Quietly, silently, the whole company disappeared within the kiosk. Under the ground, about a hundred feet up the subway track, there was a wall opening in the tunnel, which led directly into the old wine cellars. Here there was refuge from the merciless Asiatic hordes who patrolled the streets above.

No sounds entered these deep caverns from above, and the air was musty, stagnant. Candles guttered in one corner, and provisions of every description, which Jimmy Christopher, Z-7 and Tim had foraged early that morning were piled high. There were tins of canned salmon, canned corned beef, canned milk and fruit juices, as well as boxes of crackers and stores of other groceries.

Beside them, Operator 5 had knocked together a rude wooden table upon which he had placed electrical materials picked out of a wrecked wholesale warehouse. He and Tim were working on the construction of a wireless sending equipment with which to communicate with General Falk and the outside world.

Jimmy smiled as he saw the expressions of astonishment and pleasure on the faces of the refugees.

"If you ladies," he suggested gaily, "will go to work on the groceries, you may be able to scare up a meal for all of us. If you're as hungry as I am, those cans ought to go fast."

The women welcomed the chance to do something that would take their minds from the tragedy of the sacked city, and they were soon busying themselves with can-openers, chatting animatedly among themselves.

Jimmy Christopher drew the men of the group to one side, and while Tim Donovan and Z-7 listened, he spoke swiftly, keeping one eye on the three Asiatic captives, whose wounds were being tended by some of the other women.

"You men are going to be the nucleus of the fight to drive the Leopard from the city and from the country," he told them. "We'll use this place as headquarters, and we'll go about the city in search of more refugees and of weapons to arm them with. Wherever you find white men and women in hiding, you will try to guide them here in safety. We—"

"Just a minute," one of the men interrupted. "How are we going to go around the city, without being caught by these Asiatics? The minute we walk out—even if it's at night—we'll be spotted!"

"We're going to minimize that chance," Jimmy told him grimly. "Well go out only at night, as you say—"

"But they'll have flares up. They'll be able to tell us from their—"

"No they won't. Tonight, only six of us will go out. We'll be dressed just like them! There's complete equipment for six of us on the captured soldiers—even including the motorcycles. We'll be an Asiatic patrol!"

THE BOLDNESS of Jimmy Christopher's proposal stunned his listeners for a moment. There were fifteen men in that group. Some of them were downtown business employees—insurance agents, bank tellers, stockbrokers' clerks. Others were husky laborers from the fruit markets, and petty East Side gangsters. Two or three were fairly prosperous business men from other sections of the city, who had been caught in restaurants with their wives and children by the sudden bombardment. All of them, Jimmy Christopher knew, were exempt from military service either by reason of some physical disability such as heart trouble or defective eyesight, or by reason of employment in an industry necessary to the conduct of the war. The trenches in Europe had already claimed the best of American manhood, and these were but pitiable tools with which to work.

Yet he saw by the eagerness which grew in their eyes as the possibilities of his plan opened up before them, that they would work with him to the limit. All nationalities were represented in this group—they were men whose parents or grandparents or great-grandparents had come from the four corners of the earth. But they were Americans. Theirs was the stock which had brought the country to the pinnacle of its power; and when catastrophe threatened, they would fight to the last breath in their body.

A quick murmur of enthusiasm ran through the crowd. They

surrounded Jimmy, throwing questions at him, each volunteering to be among the first six to man the motorcycles that night.

Operator 5 ran his eye over them, and selected four likely-looking men.

None of them knew who he was, but they all were ready to trust themselves to his leadership. The four men selected grinned with pride at being chosen.

Jimmy detailed others to the task of stripping the armor and weapons from the dead and wounded Asiatics. Then he took a census of the weapons in the possession of the group, and found that there was only one revolver among them all.

The man who owned the revolver, he stationed at the foot of the subway stairs, with instructions to keep a lookout there. The possibility of discovery was very slight; but, like a good general, Jimmy guarded against it

Then he drew aside the four men he had selected, and spoke to them in low tones.

"We'll start tonight, as soon as it gets dark. I'll drive one motorcycle, and this gentleman—" he nodded toward Z-7—"whom you can call Mr. Smith, will drive another. You, Green—" he addressed one of the four, a stocky man of forty who was clad in the greasy overalls of a mechanic, and who knew all about motorcycles—"will drive the third. You three—Hadley, Cohen and O'Ryan—will man the side cars and use the machine guns—in case we get in a jam. Mr. Smith and I will show you how they work before we leave. Our object—"

Tim Donovan, who had been listening on the fringe of the group, broke in heatedly:

"Hey, Jimmy! Where do I come in on this? Why can't I drive the third motorcycle? I—"

"You stay here, Tim!" Jimmy told him sternly, pointing at the pile of electrical supplies. "Your job is to build a sending set before morning. You've got everything you need right there, and it's vital that we have some means of communicating with General Falk."

"But—!"

"Sorry, Tim, but the answer is—nix!"

TIM DONOVAN made a wry face, but refrained from further protest. He realized the importance of building a sending set, and he knew that he was probably the only one there, outside of Jimmy Christopher himself, who could do it. Many times he had puttered about in the laboratory which Jimmy maintained at his father's house, and he had taken a keen interest in wireless, learning everything that Jimmy tried to teach him. Though he was barely out of his middle teens, his fund of information on many subjects was equivalent to that of an expert.

"Okay, Jimmy," he said. "I'll get to work."

He left the group, and Operator 5 went on with his instructions. "Our object will be to cruise the city, avoiding large Asiatic patrols if possible. We will try to locate as many refugees as we can, and direct them to this place. If we should meet any isolated motorcycles, we will try to capture them, and thus increase our strength. We will always cruise together; if we should be recognized and chased by a superior force, we will separate, and return here by different routes, singly. In that way, the chances of all of us being caught will be reduced. *Under no circumstances* is any of you to come back here unless you're absolutely certain that you have shaken off pursuit. This place must remain a secret!"

As he finished issuing his instructions, one of the women came over, smiling, to inform them that dinner was served.

The whole tone of the group was different now from what it had been an hour before. Their spirits were soaring with the prospect of action.

And one of the men, raising his improvised cup, offered a toast:

"Here's to us—the Minute Men of 1936!"

A low shout went up from all of them, and the cups were drained. Eyes glowed, talk bubbled. The spirit of 1776 was rumbling through the vaulted spaces of the old wine cellar!

CHAPTER 10
TOWERS OF TERROR

THE DISEMBARKING of the hordes of Asiatic troops took most of the morning. While it went on, the Leopard pushed up as far as Thirty-Fourth Street. Here he found the Sixty-ninth Regiment Armory standing undamaged, and he made it his headquarters.

On the way up town, the yellow soldiers had rounded up several hundred homeless refugees, driving them from "L" stations and other places where they had hidden.

When the long column of mailed troops halted at noon time, the captives were forced to cook for the soldiers, in the improvised kitchens set up in the streets. Others were made to wait on the invaders. At the least sign of unwillingness, at the slightest mistake, death came painfully—by means of a bayonet in the stomach. The iron heel of the conqueror was making itself felt....

Down at the docks, the captured seamen and marines from the thirty-odd American ships which had surrendered were compelled to unload large square plates of metal, of material similar to the armor of the yellow soldiers. After the metal plates came heavy crates of mysterious machinery. All of this had to be hauled through the streets to the Leopard's headquarters and since it was impossible for trucks to drive through the shell-torn thoroughfares, the prisoners were pressed into service as beasts of burden. And if a man dropped and could not rise again, he met a lingering, painful death.

At last, the machinery reached Thirty-fourth Street, but the prisoners were given no respite. They were at once set to work at putting together the plates, fastening them with heavy threaded bolts which fitted into slots in the metal. Others were ordered to unpack the crates of machinery.

Supervising all the work was a wizened, wrinkle-faced Chinese, whom the yellow officers addressed as Doctor Fu. So hard did Doctor Fu drive the conscript labor, that within two hours the work was completed, and there stood, in the street before the armory, a tall, square tower, with loopholes through which projected long-barreled objects resembling guns.

The prisoners could guess, however, that these were not ordinary guns, for instead of having breeches which could be loaded, there was merely a long piston-like ramrod, worked by a lever. At a shift of the lever, the ramrod could drive into the long barrel of the tube. Just within that tube, where the ramrod struck, was a chamber containing powder, and an aluminum ball about six inches in diameter. These balls were apparently hollow, for they weighed almost nothing.

It was shortly after noon that the first counter-attack against the invaders was launched by the United States forces under General Falk. It took the shape of a small flotilla of airplanes which flew over Manhattan Island, reconnoitering.

From outside, in the street, the prisoners watched the droning planes overhead, almost hoping that the aviators would drop heavy explosives upon them and though ending their own misery, wipe out these yellow warriors who were a grisly threat against American ideals and liberty. Manhattan Island was a shambles anyway; an air bombardment could not do much further damage, and it would destroy most of the Asiatic troops massed in the streets. But no bombs were dropped....

FOR SUDDENLY, while the planes were still north of Manhattan, the long tubes in the tower began to belch flame as they were fired. The aluminum balls were catapulted upward at amazing velocity, bursting among the planes.

And abruptly, though no direct hits had been scored, the pilots seemed to lose control of their machines. Formations broke. Wings grazed, and ships crashed.

Those planes which were not destroyed at once turned tail and fled. It was the last air attack attempted by the beleaguered United States forces.

But the long guns in the metal tower did not cease firing. The American captives, watching with sinking hearts, saw that the elevation of the muzzles was being changed, saw a second tier of guns in the tower, longer than the first, swing into action.

And then they saw a part of the Asiatic column start to move northward again. Motorcycles barked and stuttered as rank upon rank of yellow troops swung into motion, drove past them.

They saw the Leopard standing in the entrance of the armory, watching his hordes move on to the attack. There were among them many who would gladly have leaped upon that figure if they had possessed a weapon of any sort. But they had been stripped of everything in their possession; and, moreover, a double rank of mailed warriors was lined up between them and the coolie conqueror.

Black anger suddenly shone in the eyes of the prisoners, as they saw a dapper figure in naval officer's uniform come out of the armory and join the Leopard. Some of them knew that man. It was Lieutenant Earl Ward.

Ward spoke a few words respectfully to the Leopard, who grinned wolfishly, nodded, and reentered the armory, with the American lieutenant trailing him.

Murmurs ran among the captives. They all wore hangdog, ashamed expressions. They could not understand what had happened to them aboard their ships. They could not understand now why they had abruptly hauled down their flags, meekly surrendered to the enemy more than thirty first-class fighting ships, all superbly equipped. They only knew that they had done a shameful thing, and they burned to vindicate themselves.

But their captors seemed to understand their mood completely, and they were given no opportunity to attempt anything. They were ringed by a circle of glittering steel bayonets in the hands of merciless yellow soldiers who did not hesitate to use them.

Now a little food was passed among them, the remains of the repast of the Asiatic troops. And then they were once more put to work.

More plates were fastened together, more machinery lifted into place by the labor of their sweating backs. But this time, the tower which they constructed was built upon a platform of steel which in turn rested on wheels. It was a mobile fort.

They were driven to their task as long as daylight lasted, and by the time night had fallen, the moving tower was complete. Then they were allowed to sleep—out in the street wherever they dropped, too weary from exhaustion to quibble at the hardness of their bed, or at their lack of covering….

IN THE meantime, the word had flashed over the entire United States that New York was destroyed. The country was in a panic of excitement. Criticism of the General Staff, of the Secretary of War, of the President, was rife.

Washington was a beehive of feverish activity. Orders crackled over the wires across the length and breadth of the country. In every training camp in the East, raw, untrained men were rushed into trains and motor trucks, headed for New York.

General Falk, who had recovered consciousness from Jimmy Christopher's blow, was once more his old dynamic self. From his headquarters at White Plains he ordered the disposition of all the American troops available. Almost a hundred thousand men were strung out across Westchester County in New York, and across Bergen and Essex Counties in New Jersey. These men were not the highly trained troops which the United States had sent to Europe, but they were far more eager to fight—because this was really a war for the protection of their homeland.

With a shrewd eye to a pitched battle, Falk had concentrated the bulk of his force around Kensico Dam, as he had told Jimmy he would do. The terrain here was ideal for defense, and there was not much doubt in General Falk's mind that he would be able to stem the advance of the Asiatic horde. All of southern Westchester County had been evacuated up to White Plains. Supplies of every kind had been withdrawn. Throughout the day huge trucks, driven by volunteer civilians, had removed from that section all the food and useful supplies which could be found. Stores and warehouses were emptied.

When the invader marched north from New York, he would find nothing to eat. Heavy cannons were being moved into place which would lay down a devastating barrage. Forts Slocum and Schuyler were crammed with ammunition for their big guns, ready to join the barrage at the zero hour. And the zero hour would be, according to Falk's plan, when the Asiatic troops reached Yonkers and Mount Vernon. He was prepared to sacrifice those towns deliberately—to wipe them from the map—and with them, the handful of yellow invaders from the East.

As a feeler, he ordered four squadrons of planes into the air, to observe the movements of the enemy in Manhattan. From the roof of the County Building in White Plains he watched the flight of those squadrons, watched them destroy themselves just as the naval planes had done the day before.

He waited in vain for a single plane to return—to report exactly what had happened. None returned. But he heard the dull booming reports of guns from New York City. He didn't know about the metal tower.

Suddenly, all the snap and pep went out of him. The same uncanny power which had made Winston surrender, was reaching out for the peppery old Chief of Staff. With sagging shoulders, Falk descended from the roof, made his way to a room in the County Building where a telegraph operator sat at a key, alertly waiting.

"Have you picked up anything from Operator 5 yet?" Falk asked anxiously.

The telegraph operator shook his head. "No, sir."

"Watch for his code signal," Falk ordered. "If he isn't dead yet, he'll manage to communicate with us somehow. He is our only hope!"

He went into his own office to report by telephone to Washington. His report was never given out to the press....

CHAPTER 11
THE LEOPARD HOLDS COURT

IN NEW YORK CITY, in the armory on Thirty-Fourth Street, the Leopard was holding court. He sat at the desk of the former commanding officer of the armory, which had been hauled out of the office into the large assembly room. Light from dozens of tapers fell on the Leopard's brutish, powerful face.

He was well satisfied with himself and with the progress of

the invasion. As he sat there, runners entered every few minutes, to report further advances of the mailed troops into Westchester.

One messenger entered, breathless, saluted, and spoke swiftly: "Master, Colonel Dato reports complete victory. The American troops encamped around the dam at Kensico are in flight. The Colonel bid me tell you that he used Doctor Fu's magic which is shot from the towers. Thousands of them were easily slaughtered, and General Falk, who commanded them, has been captured. He is being sent here to grace one of your cages!"

The Leopard smiled, and waved to the runner. "Go and eat," he ordered. "Then rest. You have done well."

He turned to the parchment-faced, shriveled old Doctor Fu, who sat at his right, clad in a silk jacket and skull cap. He nodded in satisfaction. "The country is ours," he said. "They cannot stand against the magic of your science, Fu."

The wizened old doctor made no reply, merely smiled tightly.

The Leopard glanced up at the man who stood at his left. This man still wore the uniform of a naval lieutenant in the United States Navy. He was Earl Ward.

"Now, Ward," said the Leopard, "we can question these prisoners." He glanced at a row of a dozen captives facing the desk, under guard of a file of Asiatic soldiers with fixed bayonets.

"You will be my interpreter," he told the lieutenant. Ward smirked, and bowed….

AMONG THE prisoners was Admiral Stanley Winston. The admiral's face was haggard, his eyes filled with misery at the thing he had done. He stood erect, shoulders back, facing the desk. And his eyes never left the face of Lieutenant Earl Ward.

Also in the line of captives was a gray-haired man with a bandaged head, and a chestnut-haired, blue-eyed girl, who solicitously supported the gray-haired man, with an arm about his shoulders. The man reached up and gently removed the girl's arm from about his shoulders.

"It's all right, Diane," he said softly. "I'm not an invalid any more. I can stand without help."

Diane's troubled eyes swung to glance at him sideways as she stood in the line facing the giant Leopard. "Don't exert yourself too much, dad," she whispered. "That wound in your head isn't healed yet." Her tone changed quickly to one of worry. "I wonder—" her voice dropped an octave lower—"if Katerina will be safe where we hid her." She shuddered. "I hate to think of her fate if the Leopard's men should find her while they're patrolling."

"Shhh!" Jimmy's father cautioned her. His eyes were on the Leopard, who had raised his coarse face, whispered something to Ward.

The lieutenant nodded servilely, and pointed at Admiral Winston, whose uniform was bedraggled, clotted with dirt and mud, so that it was hard to determine his rank.

Two Asiatic soldiers stepped up behind him at a gruff order from the Leopard, seized the Admiral by the arms, and pushed him forward toward the desk.

The Leopard whispered a question to Ward, who interpreted it to Winston.

"Have you any idea where Operator 5 could have gone to after he escaped from the *Dakota?*"

Winston's gaze burned into the face of his treacherous former assistant. His voice came hoarsely, huskily, filled with emotion.

"You Judas! You put some sort of drug in my coffee! Tell that dirty coolie emperor of yours that he better look out—you may do the same for him some day, if he trusts you the way I did!"

Ward's eyes lowered before the accusing glance of his former chief. He bit his lip, said: "Answer my question!"

"Go to hell!" exclaimed Admiral Winston.

The lieutenant hesitated a moment, then bent and spoke in the Leopard's ear. The big coolie bared his stained teeth in a snarl, spoke quickly, angrily.

Ward smiled thinly, straightened, and interpreted the Leopard's words with vicious vindictiveness.

"The emperor says that he is sparing you now only because of your rank. He likes to collect ex-generals, ex-kings, ex-dukes and ex-admirals of the countries he conquers. He keeps them in small steel cages, where they cannot stand up, but must remain perpetually in a crouching position. He has eleven such cages on board one of the ships in the harbor. In those cages he has a Manchukuan emperor, two Russian commissars, and the president of Finland. He instructs me to tell you that you are to join that noble collection of his. After a while, you will forget all about your pride, and beg for something to eat every day when the keeper comes around with food!"

Winston paled, and his hands clenched at his sides. But he said nothing. At an imperious motion from the Leopard, the two soldiers who held him dragged him from the room.

Two more soldiers stepped up, and pushed forward the next

in line of captives. This was a huge, bearded man, with a thick, bull neck, and shoulders whose corded muscles rippled across his shoulders, under his coat.

Ward asked him a number of questions which apparently were routine, and which were asked of each prisoner. "What is your name?"

The man's thick eyebrows came together as he frowned, and answered reluctantly: "John Shoomacher."

"What is your occupation?"

"I'm a professional wrestler."

WARD SMILED, stooped and interpreted to the Leopard, whose eyes gleamed wickedly, sizing up the captive. The emperor turned to the silent Doctor Fu, at his left, and spoke to him in Cantonese. "This man looks very powerful, Fu."

The wizened Chinese doctor bobbed his head. "I am sure he is not as strong as the Leopard!"

Ward was proceeding with the usual questions.

"The emperor is very anxious to find three people who were here in New York when the bombardment started. If you can give him any information about them, your life will be spared, and you will be given a handsome reward. These people were a very fat man named Dmitri Osman, a woman named Lina Cavelli, and a beautiful Russian girl by the name of Katerina Saratoff. Have you ever heard those names?"

John Shoomacher glared at Ward from under his thick eyebrows. He growled: "I want none of your rewards. I wouldn't tell you if I knew. And what that Admiral said to you goes for me too. You can go to hell, you Judas!"

Ward shrugged, and interpreted.

The Leopard's eyes blazed. He turned to Doctor Fu, spoke again in Cantonese, his voice rising uncontrollably.

"Fu, I must find Katerina Saratoff! From the moment when I first set eyes upon her, I knew that she was the woman to grace the Leopard's throne—a fitting companion for the conqueror of the world. I must have her, Fu! I would give up half of my conquests to have her!"

In the line of captives, the eyes of old John Christopher flickered slightly as he listened. But his face betrayed nothing. He understood Cantonese, could talk it as well—better, perhaps, than the ignorant coolie who sat behind that desk. In his youth he had served as an American Intelligence officer in Peiping during the Boxer Rebellion, and had been assigned to the Far East for five years after that. He spoke half a dozen Asiatic dialects like a native, and it was he who had schooled his son, Operator 5, in those same languages when Jimmy Christopher was assigned to the same station which his father had covered thirty years before. Jimmy himself had spent a good deal of time in the Orient, and often in their leisure, father and son would converse in Chinese, switching from one dialect to another, in order to keep in practice.

Now, John Christopher understood the passion that drove the Leopard to search for Katerina Saratoff. This wharf-rat, this coolie who had risen from the slum quarter of Hong Kong to be the dictator of all Asia, and the potential conqueror of the world, had fallen blindly in love with the beautiful, patrician

Two guards seized Diane while a third

leveled a bayonet at her stomach!

daughter of Russian nobility. And he would never rest until he had found her.

But John Christopher's thoughts were dragged away from the subject of Katerina, as he noted the thing that was occurring now. The Leopard had spoken swiftly to Ward, while John Shoomacher, the wrestler, fidgeted from one foot to the other, already regretting the lack of restraint with which he had defied the emperor.

Ward listened intently, nodding appreciatively, then translated to Shoomacher: "The emperor wishes to know whether you think you can beat him in a hand-to-hand fight."

A slow smile spread over the wrestler's not-too-intelligent features. His eyes traveled over the well-muscled body of the Leopard, and Shoomacher's chest expanded with confidence. "I hope to tell you I can. I could lick him easy. I bet I could pin him to the floor in five minutes!"

Ward smiled in smug satisfaction. "The Leopard will give you a chance for your life. If you beat him, you go free!"

THE LEOPARD arose from behind his desk, and walked around in front, stripping off his armor. He stood there, mighty muscles rippling smoothly, dressed only in his breech-clout.

At a wave of his hand, the yellow soldiers pressed the other prisoners back out of the way, so that a space was cleared around the two men.

Shoomacher eagerly removed his coat and shirt, flexed his muscles, and grinned at the emperor.

The Leopard nodded to Ward, who snapped: "Begin!"

Shoomacher fell into a crouch, warily circled the emperor,

hands hanging loose at his sides, thick stubby fingers spread to seize a grip.

The Leopard stood erect, turning slowly as the professional wrestler moved around him. His slanting eyes never left the eyes of Shoomacher.

Suddenly the wrestler lowered his head, dove straight at the emperor's stomach. The coolie did not move by so much as an inch, but his body tautened to receive the shock of the impact

There was a dull thud as Shoomacher's head *smacked* into the abdomen of the emperor with all the weight of the heavy wrestler's body behind the lunge.

The Leopard merely grunted, and his two arms went about Shoomacher's middle and lifted the heavy man into the air as if he were a child. Then the emperor's arms contracted slowly, squeezing, squeezing, while Shoomacher's arms and legs threshed futilely in the air. The pressure against the wrestler's stomach must have been terrific, for suddenly the breath was expelled from his body in a long, agonized whistle. For a moment, his arms and legs ceased to move; and in that moment, the Leopard, with a cruel, set smile on his copper features, swung the wrestler upright, keeping one arm around his waist while he pressed with his left hand against the helpless man's chin.

Shoomacher's feet wriggled helplessly under that murderous pressure, then hung limp. His head was pushed far back, his spine was arched at an almost impossible angle. Beads of sweat gleamed on his forehead, and his eyes rolled in uncontrollable terror.

Suddenly there was a sickening, crunching snap, and

Shoomacher uttered a gurgling shriek that died in his throat. His body went limp. His spine was broken.

The Leopard let him drop carelessly to the floor, where he lay, a sprawled, broken, inert completely pitiable figure.

Doctor Fu, who had sat calmly through the spectacle, nodded benevolently, went through the motions of shaking hands with himself. "An interesting exhibition," he murmured.

The emperor laughed deep in his throat "The Leopard," he said, "has yet to meet the man he cannot break!"

He waved carelessly, and two soldiers stepped forward, picked up the still living body of the broken wrestler, carried him to the door.

"Let him lie outside," the coolie emperor ordered. "He will have time to think about the fight before he dies!"

Unconcernedly, he buckled his armor on once more. Then he stepped behind his desk, sat down with a satisfied smile. "In accordance with my oath," he said to Doctor Fu, "I will break the back of one man every day until I find Katerina Saratoff!" He motioned to Ward. "Go on with the questioning of the prisoners!"

John Christopher was next in line, and he was pushed roughly forward by the guards, while Diane watched with anxious eyes, her stomach still churning after the sight of the wrestler's broken body.

The Leopard's slant eyes studied the brave, dignified bearing of John Christopher. His lips were drawn back in a half snarl. For he recognized in the quiet fearlessness of the old man the same spirit of indomitable courage that he had found

128

in other white men—like Feodor Saratoff. And it angered this coolie wharf-rat that he could not break the spirit of such men by torturing their bodies. Innately, he knew that men such as these were superior to himself; and the knowledge produced an ungovernable rage within him, drove him to fiendish, gruesome tortures.

Now, as he gazed upon Q-6, Ward bent close to him, whispering excitedly in wretched Cantonese: "I know that man! He is the father of him whom you seek. I failed to notice him in the line with the other prisoners. But now I know him. He is the father of Operator 5!"

The Leopard stiffened, threw a triumphant side glance at Doctor Fu, who smiled benignly.

"You are very sure?" the Leopard asked softly.

"Positively!" Ward said.

"That is well. For this day's work you may ask me for anything you wish!"

"Thank you, master," Ward murmured.

The Leopard kept his eyes fixed on Q-6. "Play with him a while," he instructed his interpreter. "Let him think we do not know him. I wish to watch how he acts."

WARD NODDED, was about to address John Christopher, when the old man spoke loudly, clearly, in flowing Mandarin—a tongue which neither Ward nor the Leopard understood. He seemed to be speaking to the emperor, for he gazed directly at him. But it was the wizened Doctor Fu who started in his seat at the first sound of the noble language which he had not heard spoken in years. And John Christopher was speaking to Doctor

Fu, though he looked at the Leopard. He used the bombastic, rounded sentences of the old Chinese court, where learned conversation in stilted phrases had been the popular pastime for centuries before China passed into the hands of war-lords and bandits.

"O learned man," he said. "O noble descendant of the House of Han. Are you, too, one of those who has stepped into the gutter to serve a rat of the T'angs who has raised his head from the filth of those whom you once scorned? And do you so soon forget your friends? Do you not recall the days when the Manchu emperor glittered in brocade and silk among his sparkling courtiers in the court at Peiping? I was there, my friend, and you were there. You were the court astrologer, but you were also a man of science, widely read, and replete with knowledge. Do you not recall the service I did you when the emperor was angry with you, and ordered you beheaded? I saved you then. I call upon you now to pay your debt!"

There was no expression on the face of the Chinese scientist, but his narrow, watery eyes blinked a little.

The Leopard frowned, glanced up at Ward, then turned to Doctor Fu. "He speaks in Mandarin, does he not?" the emperor asked, in Cantonese.

Fu nodded. "He is a master of the noble language of the scholars."

"What does he say?"

"He says," Fu lied, "that he is a man of honor, and he knows that you are aware of his identity."

"Does he speak Cantonese?"

"Assuredly. He has lived much in the East, he says, and speaks many languages."

"Then I will speak with him!" The Leopard addressed John Christopher. "Man, you are the father of him to whom Katerina Saratoff came, sent by her brother. I must know where she is. You will tell me—or you will scream for a quick death!"

John Christopher smiled. "You are wrong," he said quietly. "I will neither talk, nor will I scream."

The Leopard half rose in his seat, his face livid. "Three inches of bayonet in your groin will make you sing a different song!" He raised his hand to a guard. "The bayonet! But be careful not to pierce a vital organ! Twist it—"

He stopped as Doctor Fu laid a hand on his arm. "Wait!" commanded the old doctor.

The Leopard turned on him questioningly. "Well?"

"I have served you well, have I not, O Leopard? I have given into your hands the weapon which defeats your enemies before they strike a blow, have I not?"

The emperor frowned. "You have. It is true. But why do you speak of it now? Your rewards shall be great—"

"I have never asked a favor of you before. I ask one now."

"Name it!"

"I ask for the life of this man!"

"What! You are mad, Fu! He knows where Katerina Saratoff is. I must make him speak—if I cut him to bits!"

"I ask you for his life," Fu persisted. "Will you grant it if I tell you another way to make him speak?"

"Another way? You mean the way you made Feodor Saratoff speak?"

"No, I have no more of the fluid in the vial. The way I will show you is much surer."

The Leopard glanced at the skinny doctor suspiciously, but he nodded. "How?"

Fu pointed a long, crooked finger at Diane Elliot, who was standing in line with the other captives. "That girl. I observed her before. She is very close to this man. I noted from the way he talked to her that he loves her almost as a father. If you will but turn the bayonet on her, I am sure he will speak—"

John Christopher had heard every word of what the doctor had said. He broke in hoarsely: "Fu! You are a devil! You have violated the memory of your ancestors! You have betrayed one who did you a great service—"

Doctor Fu shrugged. "I have paid my debt. I owed you a life, and I have given it to you. The debt does not extend to this girl; she was not even in the world when I knew you in Peiping!"

Q-6 stood, speechless at the logic of the Chinese scientist. It was the Eastern fatalism, the disregard for human beings as such. Fu did not consider the agony of soul that he was inflicting on John Christopher. He was paying his debt to the letter.

At a swift order from the vilely grinning Leopard, two guards seized Diane, while a third leveled a bayonet at her stomach. She attempted to struggle in their grip, but was helpless.

John Christopher cried out: "Wait! Wait! You must not do that! I know nothing of my son's whereabouts!"

"I do not ask you that," the Leopard said. "I ask you where

132

I can find Katerina Saratoff. If you know, you will talk. If you do not know, then it is too bad; for you will witness the disemboweling of this beautiful young lady whom you love more than yourself!"

CHAPTER 12
RAID ON THE LEOPARD'S DEN

THREE ARMORED motorcycles chugged north on Fifth Avenue. Their spotlights lanced long furrows up the street ahead, limning the deep pits where shells had gouged out the concrete.

They proceeded slowly, like the other patrols of Asiatic troops in the conquered city. But the occupants of those cycles were not Asiatics. In the driver's seat of the leading machine sat Jimmy Christopher, and beside him, in the side car was a young American by the name of Max Cohen. The second cycle was manned by Z-7 and Bert Hadley, while in the third rode Joe Green, with Pat O'Ryan at the machine gun.

Minute Men. They were casting their lives upon the gaming table of fate as the stakes in a desperate game to learn the secret of the Leopard's power. Earlier that evening, Jimmy Christopher and Max Cohen had reconnoitered the enemy's position, learned that he had established headquarters at the armory. Now they were going to try getting inside.

Tim Donovan had succeeded in establishing contact by wireless with the main body of United States troops at Kensico under General Falk; and the newly raised hopes of the refugees

133

in the old wine cellar had been dashed at the news of Falk's capture and the precipitate route of the American forces.

Now it became imperative to pierce the enemy's stronghold and try to wrest his secret from him. The faces of all six men were grim, tight. Several times they passed other patrols, and slowed up, while Jimmy, carefully keeping his face in the shadow, had carried on a short conversation with the Asiatic soldiers in Cantonese. If there was a diversity of accent, it was not noticed, for these soldiers of the Leopard were recruited from every part of the Orient, and there were many dialects and many accents among them. Cantonese seemed to have been adopted as their official language.

From these conversations, Jimmy Christopher learned that the Leopard was questioning prisoners himself, in an effort to find if anyone had seen or heard of Katerina Saratoff. He also learned that every patrol had been charged with the task of finding her, and that a princely reward would be paid to the motor-cycle team that was successful.

At Thirty-Fourth Street the small cavalcade turned east and pulled up at a side entrance of the armory. It was quite dark here, and Jimmy felt that they could risk showing themselves. The only thing that could betray them was a glimpse of their faces, which were distinctly not Asiatic, but the helmets afforded them some security from that danger.

At a signal from Operator 5, they all dismounted, approached the entrance.

Two guards were stationed here, and dozens of yellow soldiers swaggered about. Across the street hundreds of captives, men and women, were huddled in a close group, resting on the hard concrete, while guards watched them with rifles ready. These prisoners had labored until every muscle of their bodies ached. Now they were waiting to be questioned.

Jimmy Christopher marched to the doorway of the armory at the head of his small company, striding boldly as if he had business inside. The guard, recognizing the insignia of a petty officer on his breastplate, saluted, and stood aside.

NUMEROUS YELLOW soldiers were moving about within, bent on various missions. The six Americans made their way along a corridor, turned left toward the main assembly room. Suddenly, Operator 5 stopped stock still, his face set and cold. His eyes had met the eyes of another man—who was being marched out of the assembly room between two soldiers! They recognized each other….

It was Admiral Stanley Winston, being taken from the presence of the Leopard. Winston half-opened his mouth to utter an exclamation, then shut it again.

Jimmy Christopher whispered to the others: "After them boys! But take it easy. And keep your heads down!"

They followed Winston and his two guards to the other end of the armory, and down a flight of stairs. The two guards paid no attention.

Down below were the detention cells, and into one of these the guards were about to thrust Winston. Jimmy Christopher glanced around, saw that there was no one else in the cellar, and exclaimed:

"Now boys!"

He leaped at the startled guards, lunging with his bayonet. Z-7, beside him, did likewise. So efficiently had it been done, that no sound was made.

The other four Minute Men dragged the two dead guards into the cell, stripped them of armor and weapons, while Jimmy Christopher and Z-7 spoke to Winston.

The admiral exclaimed: "Operator 5! How did you get here?"

"Never mind!" Jimmy said hurriedly. "There's no time for explanations. We're here to find some clue to the Leopard's secret. Can you help us?"

Winston shook his head. "I know as little as I did yesterday. I know that Ward doctored my coffee in some way. It was my fault that the fleet was destroyed. I should have listened—"

Jimmy stopped the admiral, said: "Put on that suit, sir. It'll get you by."

While Winston was donning the armor, he spoke quickly: "Your father's up there in the assembly room, Operator 5. It'll be his turn to be questioned in a few minutes. There's a girl with him—"

"One?" Jimmie queried anxiously.

"Yes. Very pretty, with chestnut hair—"

"Diane!" Z-7 exclaimed. "Then he hasn't caught Katerina yet?"

"No. But he's torturing the prisoners to make them talk. God!" Winston's voice was tense with emotion. "I only want one chance at that Leopard—and at Earl Ward. Ward's his interpreter."

Jimmy swung around. "Let's go! We're going to take a crack at the Leopard!"

He hurried back up the stairs. The entrance to the cellar was on the Thirty-third Street side, and he stopped, his eyes narrowed, looking down a corridor at right angles to the one they had used.

A LONG line of Asiatic soldiers was moving along this corridor through the main entrance of the building. And they were passing, one at a time, into a room, the door of which was wide open. From where the Americans stood, they could see into that room, which was lit by a half-dozen candles. Four Chinese, in white smocks, were in that room, and as the soldiers entered, the white-smocked Celestials picked up hypodermic syringes from tables at their elbows, swabbed off the arm of a soldier, and drove home the plunger of the hypo.

They were giving some sort of injection to the men as fast as they could work.

"I think, Chief," Operator 5 whispered, "that we're on the track of the Leopard's secret!" His eyes were fixed on a small room next to the laboratory, the door of which was also open. In this room, two more white-smocked Asiatics were working over test tubes set in brackets above Bunsen burners. While Jimmy and Z-7 watched, one of these two poured the contents of the test tubes into a large vial, and carried it out into the laboratory in which the injections were being given. There was only one man left in the small room, and Jimmy said hurriedly:

"Z-7! I'm going to get one of those!"

Without waiting for acknowledgment Operator 5 swiftly entered the small room. The white-coated Chinese looked up inquiringly, peering near-sightedly through his thick-lensed

Jimmy's automatic barked. Four men fell to four shots!

glasses. He started in consternation as he realized that Jimmy was not an Asiatic. But Operator 5 gave him no chance to cry out.

Stepping in close, he brought up his fist in a swift, hard blow to the man's chin, sent him smashing back against the wall, unconscious. Then he swung quickly to the row of tubes above the Bunsen burner, removed them, and poured their contents into a vial. He corked it, sped out of the room to join Z-7 again.

"Let's get away from here, quick!" he urged. He led the way down the corridor. No alarm was raised....

Jimmy hurried in the direction of the assembly room, with Z-7 beside him, and Winston and the Minute Men behind.

They came in sight of the large double doors, and Z-7 shouted suddenly: "God! Jimmy! Look at that! Diane!"

The tableau caused Jimmy's blood to race. The Leopard was seated at the desk. In front of the desk, stood his father, in the grip of two guards. Close by, two more Asiatics were gripping Diane while a third was drawing back a bayonet to plunge it into her body.

Jimmy Christopher flung himself forward, headlong, his automatic snapping into his hand as if by magic. The guard with the bayonet was just lunging toward Diane when Jimmy's first hasty shot caught him high in the chest.

John Christopher turned toward the corridor. Numerous Asiatics now swung toward the doorway, raising their rifles, but Jimmy's automatic spoke quickly in sharp, staccato barks. A deadly calm was upon him. Each shot was placed perfectly. Four men fell to four shots. They were the huge guards who pinioned Diane and John Christopher. Above the reverberations of the swift reports, Jimmy shouted loudly: "Diane! Dad! Run! This way!"

JOHN CHRISTOPHER leaped into action at the sound of his son's voice, seized Diane by the hand and raced with her through the doorway, then dragged her flat on the floor as the rifles in the room began to crack spitefully.

Operator 5 had held his fire during that tense moment while his father and Diane raced from the room.

Now Diane and John Christopher were safe, and the doorway was clear. The Minute Men raised their own rifles, poured out a withering blast.

John Christopher had urged Diane on again, and Jimmy gestured his men on down the corridor. They raced around an angle in the passageway and out into the night through the side door they had entered.

The Oriental guards died without understanding what had killed them.

Outside, the motorcycles were still parked where Jimmy and his men had left them. They all piled in, Diane, Q-6 and Admiral Winston each crowding into a sidecar with one of the Minute Men.

The soldiers in the street were dazed by the unexpected swiftness of the escape. For a moment, they did not realize that the armored men were not their Asiatic comrades. And that moment of respite was sufficient for the Americans.

After a few minutes of breakneck speed, Jimmy raised a hand, pointed south, and they raced downtown.

Through the night, along broken streets, Jimmy Christopher led his tiny army at a reckless pace. Behind them in the armory, the Leopard, livid and choking with rage, was spluttering orders, threats, curses. Every motorcycle available was ordered out to hunt the fugitives.

But the Minute Men had a good start, and a brilliant commander. They shook the pursuit easily, and in twelve minutes they were holed up in the old wine cellar.

Tim Donovan let out a boyish whoop of joy when he saw Diane and Q-6. But Jimmy permitted little time for greetings. He drew Z-7 and Tim Donovan aside. "Any more news, Tim?" he questioned.

Tim nodded. "I did what you told me, Jimmy. I got through to Washington, and talked to the Secretary of War. He's at his wits' end—a regular blue funk. He orders you to report to him in person—at once. He has called the North Beach Airport, and has arranged for a seaplane to be waiting for you in the East River, without lights, at midnight. You're to get out to it tonight. The Secretary wants you in Washington too, Z-7. The plane will hold two people besides the pilot."

"All right," Jimmy said. "I have to go anyway. I want to get to a laboratory as fast as I can, and analyze the contents of this vial. These people will be safe."

For a moment he stood deep in thought. Then he called over Admiral Winston, explained to him what he was going to do. "You're the logical man to take charge of this secret headquarters, Winston. Keep these people safe in here. Don't let them venture out again. The Asiatics are surely combing the city for us."

Winston's eyes held a wistful light. "Do you feel confident that I can be trusted with a command of any kind, Operator 5, after the way—?"

"Nonsense," Z-7 cheered him heartily, clapping him on the back. "Look at what happened to Falk. You couldn't help it. Operator 5 and I know you're all right."

IT WAS plainly visible to them both how Winston's shoulders suddenly straightened, and how his chin rose and jutted. He had been bitterly reproaching himself as a coward—a traitor, almost. The confidence in him which Jimmy had shown by placing him in charge of these people had given him faith in himself.

Jimmy hurried over to Diane and his father, managed to pull them away from the eager, curious men and women about them. "Where is Katerina Saratoff?"

Diane exchanged glances with John Christopher, then informed Jimmy quickly: "When the shells began to fall near Mercy Hospital, we moved all the patients out on stretchers. Dad was able to walk by then, and he and I and Katerina helped. After the bombardment, the Sixth Avenue L Station at Fourteenth Street was still standing, so we moved into it. Two patients died while we were in the station. Then we saw the Asiatics coming to round up prisoners, and dad here said that if the Leopard got Katerina, she would be worse off than any of us. So we put her on a stretcher and covered her with a sheet, alongside of the two who had previously died. When the soldiers came, dad told them that they were the bodies of smallpox cases, and the Asiatics left them severely alone. So Katerina is probably still up there."

"Good work, Diane," Jimmy praised her. He turned to his father. "I'm leaving here at midnight, dad. I've asked Winston to take charge. I thought it would help him get his self-confidence back." He explained about the message from the Secretary of War. "Besides, I want to analyze this stuff. If, God willing, it helps us beat these Asiatics, we'll come down on New York shooting. So help Winston keep everybody down in these vaults where they'll be safe. I'll communicate with Tim, and let you know what's going on."

John Christopher nodded. "If you stage a counter-attack, Jimmy, let me know a little ahead of time. I'll try to get to where Katerina is, and keep her safe."

CHAPTER 13
FATE CALLS THE
COOLIE EMPEROR

DAWN OF the second day following the successful raid of the Minute Men against the Leopard's stronghold in the armory found the remnants of the United States troops entrenched around the southeastern edge of Muscoot Reservoir, thirty miles north of New York City.

The vanguard of the Asiatics was less than five miles away, at Mount Kisco.

Southern Westchester and western Connecticut had been

sacked, burned and pillaged. It was now a trackless, charred wasteland.

From every part of the country, frantic queries were pouring into Washington. Why were the troops retreating without striking a blow? Why was heavy ordnance abandoned without a shot being fired? Would the whole country be given over to pillage and fire and rapine, like New York?

To all these questions, Washington had for two days maintained a discreet, painful silence.

At the Muscoot Reservoir, however, a strange spirit of animation was in the air. Peculiarly, the atmosphere of self-distrust and futility which had pervaded the American troops for the past three days was lacking. And strange things were happening there, too....

Heavily guarded supply trucks raced along all the highways, and, upon arrival at the Muscoot encampment, were unloaded with frenzied zeal and haste. On being opened, the crates were proved to contain however, not guns or other similar implements of war, but cases of bottles, outfits of hypodermic syringes, and cartons of cotton and antiseptics!

Physicians and interns by the hundreds seized the strange military material and laid it out in hastily improvised infirmaries along the reservoir.

At Headquarters, located just outside the small town of Goldens Bridge, Jimmy Christopher sat before a hurriedly installed battery of telephones. As the reports came in from the physicians in charge of each field-unit, he assigned to that unit troops for inoculation.

In a field near Jimmy's office, a plane whirred to a landing, and a few moments later, the Secretary of War strode into the room. Scowling, he strode wrathfully to the desk where Jimmy sat.

Jimmy Christopher smiled, motioned to an officer to take charge of the phones, and arose from his chair. He took the Secretary's arm, led him into the next room. Here, a laboratory had been set up—small, but complete in every detail.

"I haven't had a chance to talk to you, sir, since I came up here. I told you about the vial I had taken from the laboratory in the armory, but you didn't pay much attention to it at the time. Well, I analyzed the stuff, and found it was a compound of strychnine and caffeine. The Leopard was giving his men an injection of that stuff."

The Secretary gazed at Jimmy in a puzzled manner. "Why?"

"I couldn't understand it either," Jimmy went on, "until I analyzed some of the air in the pockets of the ground around Kensico Dam where we were defeated two days ago.

"I found a gas which I had never known to exist before. It has all the properties which would be possessed by a compound of nembutal, aconitine and sodium amytol. Those are all coma-producing drugs, but if they were to be reduced to a gaseous form they would be too volatile for any practical use. This gas which I found in the air-pocket, is a heavy gas, and yet possesses all the coma-producing qualities."

"I still don't—" the Secretary began.

But Jimmy hurried on. "Don't you understand, sir? Those towers of the Asiatics; those queer guns of theirs—it would be impossible to disseminate any ordinary gas over a vast area. But it can be done with this one. And to ensure that his own troops are not affected by it, the Leopard injects them with a stimulant of strychnine and caffeine. Thus, when that queer feeling of futility struck the navy, the Asiatics were not affected in the same way because they had already assimilated a powerful stimulant. The same thing happened at Kensico Dam."

Suddenly a light gleamed in the Secretary's eyes. "Then you're giving the same stimulant to our own men now!"

"Exactly, sir! And we'll—"

He stopped as an officer burst into the room, saluted, and reported excitedly: "The Asiatics are advancing, sir. The attack has started!"

Jimmy nodded. He said to the Secretary: "The next ten minutes will tell the story, sir. If I've guessed right—victory. If I've guessed wrong—we're doomed!"

Operator 5 hurried out of the headquarters building, issued swift orders to the officers gathered about him. To the East he could see the armored motorcycles of the Asiatics racing toward the hastily built trenches.

From a distance came the dull reports of the queer guns on the steel towers of the Asiatics. The gas shells began to burst in the air about them. The gas itself was odorless, and Jimmy gazed anxiously from one face to another of the officers about him. They had all had injections, including himself.

Z-7 came hurrying over to him, exclaimed: "Jimmy! I think you've hit it this time. I don't feel a thing!"

Jimmy nodded. "The troops all seem okay." He glanced down the line of trenches at the tense, youthful faces of the volunteer defenders, waiting for the signal to fire at the advancing motorcycles.

Suddenly Jimmy Christopher's body tautened. He gripped Z-7's arm. "Look at that, Chief!" he exclaimed.

From a side road, only a hundred yards distant, an automobile had swung into the main road in the path of the oncoming motorcycles. It was an open touring car, and Jimmy and Z-7 could see that the two occupants were both women.

"It's Diane!" Jimmy shouted. "And she's got Katerina with her!"

Behind the touring car raced a motorcycle. It was driven by an Asiatic soldier, and in the side car, standing erect, was the huge figure of the Leopard bent down to the machine gun on the side car. Flame belched from it, and a stream of bullets lanced out toward the auto, to the accompaniment of a wicked *rat-tat-tat*.

A rear tire on the automobile exploded with a report that sounded like a dull echo of the guns from the towers. The touring car careened, and Jimmy could see Diane struggling with the wheel.

The oncoming motorcycles were close now, on the main road. Diane's car lurched to one side, landed in the ditch along the road. The two white-faced girls sprang from the twisted wreckage, started to race toward the American trenches, while the Asiatic motorcycles charged down on them from behind.

At the same time, the Leopard sprang from the side car of his motorcycle, raced after the girls. His great body glistened in the morning light and he was brandishing a heavy, two-edged sword. His face was twisted in fury; his lips were drawn back from his teeth in a snarl. He was very close to the panic-stricken girls now. It was obvious that he would reach them perhaps two minutes before the roaring motorcycles of his own troops. In either event, the two girls were doomed....

JIMMY GROANED aloud. He could not give the order to the men in the trenches to shoot, for Diane and Katerina were directly in the line of fire.

"Z-7!" he shouted hoarsely. "Take over command!" And with that, he leaped up, sprinted furiously, frantically, down the road toward the three. As he ran, his automatic came into his hand, and he raised it to take a pot-shot at the Leopard. But at that instant, he saw the driver of the Leopard's sidecar rise behind his plate armor, and draw a bead with his rifle on the two fleeing girls. Jimmy swung his automatic, sent a stream of hot lead spouting at that soldier until the clip of the automatic was empty. But his shots had winged home, for the man dropped the rifle from nerveless fingers, toppled from the cycle to sprawl dead in the dusty roadway.

And just at that moment, when it seemed the girls might outrun the huge man pursuing them still, Katerina tripped, fell in the road. Diane, close behind her, barely missed stumbling over her, lost precious seconds as she bent to help.

The Leopard, now only a few paces away uttered a mad cry of triumph, raised his ponderous broadsword. Jimmy, coming from the opposite direction, covered the short space between him and the coolie emperor in a desperate breathless sprint, clubbed his automatic, flung it violently into the Leopard's face!

That blow probably would have killed any ordinary man, but the giant coolie shook his head, plunged ahead....

Jimmy stood weaponless now, and the Leopard grinned evilly, advanced toward him with the sword raised aloft for a slicing, slanting blow which could shave a man's head from his neck.

Operator 5 waited until the sword was actually descending before he acted. Then, with the swiftness of light, he dropped flat to the ground while the blade whistled harmlessly over his head.

The Leopard was pulled off balance, by the weight of the sword at that instant, and Jimmy launched himself from the ground in a short football tackle which toppled the huge man sideways.

Like a majestic forest giant falling before the grim hacking of the woodsman, the coolie fell heavily on his right arm. The keen edge of the sword, still gripped in his massive fists was jammed up between his shoulder and his neck. It sliced through the Leopard's thick throat as if it were cutting butter, and the conqueror of Asia—the scourge of Russia and terror of America—lay there on the road, bleeding to death....

Jimmy Christopher was back on his feet in an instant. He raced to Katerina, who was limping in the road with a badly twisted ankle, resting on Diane's arm. He picked up the Russian girl, gave Diane a shove that sent her sprawling off the road into the ditch, leaped to follow her just as the first ranks of the armored motorcycles swept up. The drivers tried frantically to brake their machines when they saw their master lying in the road bathed in his own blood. But they were traveling far too fast. Solid-tired wheels crunched on the bones of the man who had yearned to master the world….

And at that instant, Z-7, standing in front of the headquarters building, raised his arm in a signal. From the trenches lining the reservoir a solid sheet of fire belched at those motorcycles from the muzzles of a thousand rifles. The cycles piled up on one another in crashing wreckage. The road became a mess of twisted, flaming metal and writhing dying men.

A great shout of triumph rose from the trenches, and wave after wave of young men went over the top, charging with bayonets. They swept past the spot where Jimmy Christopher crouched with Diane and Katerina, swept around the wrecked motorcycles, swarmed down the road in a yelling, mad, victorious charge against the foot-soldiers of the Asiatics who were still a great distance in the rear.

Those Oriental troops had never encountered active resistance before. The sudden sight of the charging madmen of the American army signified only one thing to them—that their master's magic had finally failed.

Their courage was not equal to facing that on-sweeping charge. They turned tail and ran. The great Asiatic army fled in panicky rout…!

ALONG THE edge of the road, Diane was saying swiftly to Jimmy:

"I couldn't bear to think of Katerina staying alone there with the corpses. So I stole out last night, and went to the L station, and found her. We wandered over to the Express Highway, and saw that touring car, abandoned. I started it, and we raced up here. We didn't know that the Leopard was camped around Mt. Kisco, and they sighted us."

Diane was breathing quickly, her eyes shining with excitement. "And believe me, Jimmy, the Leopard almost had us!"

Jimmy saw Z-7 run past them after the charging troops, and waved to him.

From the direction of the headquarters building, the Secretary of War was sedately approaching them, his face wreathed in smiles.

Jimmy sighed. "It's a victory, all right. Those lads of ours won't stop until they've chased every last Asiatic back into the ocean again. And you, Katerina—" he glanced somberly at the pile of twisted motorcycles in the road, beneath which lay the body of the coolie who had wanted to be emperor—"and you, Katerina, are revenged for your brother."

"Yes," Katerina said simply. "Feodor must be satisfied—wherever he is. And I—well, I've found a wonderful new friend, Jimmy Christopher—the bravest man in the world!"

www.ingramcontent.com/pod-product-compliance
Lightning Source LLC
Chambersburg PA
CBHW052139170626
46812CB00004B/1510